Not likely. It must be the amnesia thing again.

"I can't remember ever going on a picnic, not once in my whole entire life. For all practical purposes, I'm a picnic virgin. That doesn't seem right for a guy my age."

In spite of herself, Sunny's lips twitched with the threat of a smile. She had trouble thinking of Dean Weylin as a *virgin* anything. A wealthy man-about-town, at twenty-three he'd been older and far more experienced than she during that marvelous summer of madness.

She eyed him suspiciously. "You've never been on a picnic?" She knew better and wondered if the memory had really escaped him. On more than one occasion that summer they had sneaked off into the hills to find a secluded spot. Not that food had been very much on their minds, of course. Theirs had been a different kind of hunger. An all-consuming passion.

A passion that led to promises...promises that could only be broken.

ABOUT THE AUTHOR

Charlotte has had bits and pieces of stories running through her head for as long as she can remember. Until recently, however, she concentrated her writing in the nonfiction area. But in her imagination, she's always produced stories of romance, which she is now delighted to share with her readers. Charlotte lives in Southern California with her husband, Chuck, and their very spoiled cat, Patches.

Books by Charlotte Maclay

HARLEQUIN AMERICAN ROMANCE

Chapter One

"Hey, mister."

H. Dean Weylin III, slowly pried open one eye. Two pairs of identical bright blue eyes stared back at him from the four-foot-high level, one pair hidden behind glasses precariously held together by a dirty strip of adhesive tape. Twins, he decided. Or else he'd had a relapse and was seeing double again.

He shifted slightly, setting into motion the hammock he'd strung between two pine trees at the campground.

"Whata ya want?" he mumbled, groggy from his midday nap in the sun.

"Mom needs help."

Instinctively Dean was wide-awake, years of training driving him to instant alertness. He swung his legs over the side of the hammock, stood and reached for his medical bag—

Reality slammed into him with the force of a lightning bolt. "What kind of help?" For the last nine months he'd hardly been able to help himself, much less a woman in trouble.

"The ladder fell over and she's stuck on the roof," the towhead with the glasses said.

"It's too heavy for us to lift," his brother explained. "She said we should go find a man."

Dean supposed he qualified. Given the situation, he might even be able to provide some assistance. "Where is she?"

"At our place. Up the hill."

Dean glanced in the direction the boys indicated. As far as he knew, there was only one building up there, the Cloud High Roadhouse on the Angeles Crest Highway out of Los Angeles, a stopping-off place for a sandwich or cold glass of beer for anybody escaping the city for a quick visit to the San Gabriel mountains. Dean figured the Forest Service campground, where he had parked his van, provided the café with its closest neighbors. For the past few weeks, he'd been strongly drawn to this particular camping locale, though he couldn't have said why. The campground offered little in the way of amenities.

He'd simply felt he needed to be here.

"Come on, mister," one bright-eyed boy encouraged. "She's gonna fall if we don't get the ladder back up."

"Wouldn't want that to happen," he agreed.

He trudged up the path after the energetic twins, the five-thousand-foot altitude and months of recuperation from a gunshot wound taking its toll on Dean's lungs. The season lingered on the cusp between fall and winter, the air clean though still comfortably warm during the day, the pines and cedars the only trees showing their green. The oaks were dusty with a summer's worth of grime that would take a good rainstorm to wash away.

By the time the trio reached the top of the rise, Dean was breathing hard. Given his rotten physical condition, this mission of mercy had become more difficult than he had anticipated.

"Where's your dad?" he asked the boys.

"We don't gots one," the kid with the glasses announced over his shoulder.

"We got a great-grandpa," his brother added. "He's old."

At the first sight of a woman dangling from the roof of the roadhouse with her legs wrapped around a downspout, Dean concluded the boys' mother wasn't old. Her honey blond hair was pulled back into one of those fancy French braids. A tatty gray sweatshirt hid much of her figure, but the soft swell of her hips suggested a young woman in her prime. Long, trim legs tucked into tight-fitting jeans added to the impression.

Dean Weylin hadn't thought about a woman or sex since a gang-banger had tried to blow a rival gang member away in an emergency room and he'd been caught in the cross fire. As his body reacted to the woman hanging so precariously from the roof, Dean found it very gratifying to know *that* part of his memory hadn't been lost amid the shrapnel that had entered his brain.

"Hang on," he called, heading for the extension ladder that had fallen to the ground. "I'll get you down in a minute."

"Thirty seconds would be better," she said. "My arms are getting really tired."

"We found him, Mom. A man. Down at the campground."

"That's nice, dear."

Her voice seemed a little shaky, as if she wasn't kidding about being tired from hanging on to the roof, but was determined not to frighten her children. Dean figured he'd better hop to it.

He was still breathing hard from his hike up the hill as he hefted the ladder, an old wooden monstrosity that should have been replaced by an aluminum one years ago. It was heavy and awkward to maneuver, something more suited for use by a logger than a woman with rounded hips and slender legs. Dean wondered how she had managed to get it upright in the first place, and why she didn't have a man around to handle whatever it was she'd wanted to do up on the roof.

"Okay," he announced, tugging on the frayed rope to extend the ladder to full height, then resting it against the edge of the roof. "The ladder's right next to you. Just swing your legs over—"

"I can't. If I let go with my legs, I don't think my arms will hold me."

Dean frowned. Where was an emergency rescue team when you needed one?

"You gotta help her, mister."

"She's our mom."

He slanted the boys a glance. Somewhere he'd seen eyes that blue, but he couldn't remember where. "No sweat, kids. Just stand back so you don't get in the way.''

Grabbing a rung at shoulder level, Dean proceeded up the ladder. Given the steep cant to the overhanging roof, the stranded woman was stuck about twenty-five feet off the ground. Not all that high. If she fell, she'd probably only twist an ankle. Worse case, she'd break it. No doubt neither situation would be viewed as a convenient scenario by a woman raising two children.

Reaching her level, Dean snaked his arm around her middle.

Nice. He all but sighed at the thought.

He didn't want to register the comfortable, perfect fit of her slender waist as he embraced her. Or acknowledge the feel of her breasts resting against his forearm.

His newly awakened body had other ideas, however. He was in the middle of rescuing one sexy lady, who likely wouldn't be at all pleased to know just how instantly he responded to her... *welcomed* the feel of her as if she were a lover who had been absent for a very long time.

Her scent, a mix of alpine freshness and musky female, triggered a similar response.

He didn't know quite how to act. He wanted to cheer for a libido that hadn't gone dead, yet he was embarrassed he'd react that way to a woman whose face he'd never even seen.

Together they worked their way back down the ladder. He could tell she was shaky, muscles stressed like rubber bands stretched to the limit for too long a time.

Somewhere in his gut, he was a little wobbly, too. In his case, it had to be the altitude, he assured himself. Not the woman who he spooned against his body during their descent.

They reached the ground.

She turned, murmuring, "Thank you. I wasn't sure I could hang on much longer."

Uniquely silver-blue eyes, a blend of a bright summer sky mixed with the depth of rain clouds, looked up at Dean. About three cubic yards of high-altitude air lodged in his lungs, making breathing difficult. Undefined memories assailed him, but none of them took shape, only an odd feeling that he had discovered the reason he'd been so powerfully drawn to these particular mountains.

"Hi. I'm Dean Weylin," he said, though at some deep gut level he thought perhaps his polite self-introduction might be unnecessary. "You okay?"

Her eyes locked on his face, her lips moving without sound. Finally she nodded.

"What were you doing up there?"

The tip of her tongue peeked out and swept across the full shape of her lips. "Stringing the Christmas lights."

"Rushing the season a little, aren't you?" It wasn't yet the first of November.

"Usually we leave the lights up all year." She continued to search his face in a curiously intense examination, as though each detail was critically important. "We reroofed this summer, so the lights had to come down. I needed to get them back up before the first snow."

"That makes sense." What didn't make sense was the way electrical circuits in his brain were trying to make connections and failing. It was like a thousand tiny pinpricks of light snapping and popping inside his head, memories trying to surface but unable to find an escape route.

The boys nestled themselves up next to their mother, one on either side. In a gesture that looked as if it had been repeated thousands of times, she hooked her arms protectively around the twins. Her fierce love for them was apparent as she squeezed them tight.

"We're sorry, Mom."

"For knocking over the ladder."

"These are my sons. Howie." She indicated the boy with the glasses. "And Danny." A loving smile softened the intensity of her gaze. She ruffled Danny's curly hair. "They're known in the neighborhood as Mischief and Trouble."

"Which one's which?" Dean asked, grinning.

"When there's devilment to be done, they're as interchangeable as high-energy flashlight batteries."

"I can see that."

"Mom, can we invite Mr. Weylin in for coffee?" Howie asked. "We oughta thank him for saving your life."

"If I'd fallen, I don't think I would have actually died," their mother said sensibly.

"You might have," Howie insisted.

"We could show him our collection of Indian arrowheads," Danny suggested.

She visibly hesitated in a way that got Dean's goat. He had, after all, climbed a ladder to rescue the lady.

A cup of coffee as a reward seemed reasonable enough.

"I'm sure we've inconvenienced Mr. Weylin—"

"Call me Dean. Please."

"Hey, that's my name, too," Howie announce. "Howard Dean McCloud. That's me."

"Then we have something in common," Dean commented, his attention still on the boy's mother.

Her curiously fascinating tongue appeared again. "I'm not sure you'll find arrowheads all that interesting . . . Dean."

"Actually, Indian artifacts have always intrigued me." A small lie, he admitted, but a useful one at the moment. He didn't want to let go of the feeling that he should know this woman. And didn't. Though he had no right to be thinking about any woman in the terms he'd been considering about her. "If the coffee's no bother, Ms. . . . ?" He let the question dangle.

Responding slowly, she said tautly, "Sunny. Sunny McCloud."

A perfect name for a woman whose cheeks had colored like a rosy sunrise, either from embarrassment or, oddly enough, due to a flare of anger.

Before Dean could react, Danny grabbed his hand. "Come on, mister."

"I got a piece of smoky quartz," Howie announced, taking his other hand. "Billy's dad—he's a ranger—says we could find some gold if we look hard enough."

The boys swept Dean past an umbrella table for customers who wanted to eat outside and took him in through the front door of the roadhouse. He grinned.

They were like tiny tidal waves of energy. No wonder their mother thought of them as double trouble.

In the main dining room, antique snow sleds, old wooden skis and posters from the local ski area decorated knotty pine walls. Lacquered picnic tables with benches were placed at even intervals on the concrete floor. At one side of the room, a couple of black oil drums had been modified into a wood-burning stove that heated both the dining room and the adjacent bar.

No elegant luxury here, Dean mused, surprised to find the comfort of a mountain hideaway instead.

His young hosts parked him at a small table beside a window. A lot of running around ensued while the boys raced to find their hidden treasures, which gave Dean a chance to observe Sunny glide behind the bar to make a fresh pot of coffee. She worked with an economy of motion, her gestures simple and sure and somehow graceful in spite of the mundane task of filling the pot with water and sliding in a new filter.

Dean couldn't remember a time when he'd found the act of making coffee quite so mesmerizing. Or so naggingly familiar.

HE DIDN'T REMEMBER HER.

Sunny's hands shook as she placed the coffeepot on the warmer; her stomach knotted in a tangle of emotions she'd long ago repressed—anger, hurt, a deep sense of betrayal, and lingering vulnerability.

She'd seen a spark of masculine awareness in his gaze but no recognition in his eyes, so distinctively blue she'd always been reminded of polished agate stones.

What bitter irony that she hadn't forgotten Dean Weylin as easily as he had apparently forgotten her. But then, she had much more reason to remember.

How could fate have been so cruel as to place him nearby when the boys had gone for help? she wondered, tamping down a wild amalgam of emotions that threatened to erupt.

Except for looking a little pale, Dean hadn't changed much in the past nine years. His hair, filled with cowlicks that made it unmanageable, was still the shade of walnut shells shot through with traces of gold. Her fingers itched with the tactile memory and the futility of trying to smooth those curls.

The smile lines at the corners of his eyes had deepened a bit with age. He hadn't bothered to shave in a couple of days and his rugged jawline was rough with whiskers the same light brown color as his hair. His burgeoning beard, combined with the old flannel shirt he wore and jeans with a frayed hole in one knee, gave him the look of a bum. Sunny knew better.

H. Dean Weylin III, was the hardest working man she'd ever known. A part of her still harbored a tight coil of resentment that she hadn't been able to compete with his career.

The stream of coffee continued to fill the pot as the boys came running downstairs from their room with their prize arrowheads. Normally Howie and Danny didn't take so easily to strangers. There was no logic to their eager acceptance of Dean. None at all.

For a moment, she wished she could scoop her boys into her arms and hide them away in some safe place. But maybe she was overreacting. Even a busy man had a right to go camping in the mountains now and again. Just as a man had a right to forget a brief summer romance from his youth.

THE BOYS REAPPEARED, a handful of arrowheads clattering onto the tabletop in front of Dean.

Grabbing a small bag of potato chips from a bar display, Danny ripped open the cellophane and spilled the contents onto the table next to their youthful treasures. He ate the first chip himself.

"I got this one up at the fire lookout," Howie said. He knelt on the chair across the table and shoved an arrowhead toward Dean. "See how the tip is broken?"

"Yeah, I see," Dean dutifully responded. He kept one eye on Sunny, wishing she'd glance over her shoulder at him. But she studiously avoided looking in his direction. He liked her profile—the slight tilt to the tip of her nose, a determined chin. An intriguing combination.

"Billy's dad says that means the Indian hit somethin' with it. Maybe even *killed* somethin'. Like a deer. Or a rabbit."

"That a fact?"

"Billy's dad goes huntin' and stuff. You ever killed anything?"

"Can't say as I have." Nor did he want to. Being the target of a murderous weapon had certainly soured him on that prospect.

"Oh." A decidedly disappointed reaction from Howie.

Standing beside the table, Danny added his two cents worth. "Billy's dad can split a whole tree into kindlin' in just one day."

"He sounds like a real paragon of virtue."

Danny scowled at the possibility that Dean had no such virtues at all. "Our other friend, Mitch Standish? His dad runs the ski lift. It's neat. Sometimes he lets us ride the rope tow for free."

"Good for him."

"What do you do, mister?"

"I'm a doctor," Dean responded.

If he'd been looking for approval, he certainly wasn't going to get any from the boys. Danny wrinkled his nose. Howie plopped an elbow on the table and propped his chin on his fist.

"That mean you give kids shots and gross stuff like that?"

"Sort of." His job, what he could remember of it, had been far more complex. "But I'm not a doctor anymore. At least, temporarily I'm not."

"How come?"

"Well, I got shot."

"Shot? Like with a gun?"

Now he had their attention. "That's right."

"Wow! Where'd you get hit?"

"In the head."

He heard Sunny gasp and was sorry he'd said anything at all about the shooting.

The boys' eyes rounded, Howie's magnified several times by the thick lenses of his glasses. "Can we see?"

He touched his temple above the hairline. "Not much to see, really. An ugly scar where they stitched me back together again."

"How come you aren't dead?" Howie asked.

"Just lucky, I guess." He'd come close, though. Very close. As it was, he'd lost about everything that mattered to him.

"Boys! You're pestering the man." Sunny placed the mug in front of Dean and poured the coffee. Though it came as no surprise, hearing him talk about being shot was as painful as if the bullet had struck her instead. The newspaper article she'd read months ago had made her physically ill, even though it hadn't contained specifics about the shooting. She wasn't eager to hear the details.

"But, Mom! Didn't you hear? Dean got hit in the *head!* By a *bullet!*"

"I know, dear."

"Man, that's so neat! Wait'll we tell Billy. His dad never did nothin' like that."

"Did anything." She automatically corrected him.

"Well, he didn't," Danny repeated stubbornly.

"Boys, if you don't leave Dr. Weylin alone—"

"They're fine." Dean caught her wrist, his long tapered fingers restraining her with a light touch. He'd always been gentle. Extraordinarily so. "Can you join me for coffee?"

"No. I can't." That's how it had all started nine years ago. Sunny knew enough to not want to repeat that particular lesson. "This time of year we get a small rush around dinnertime. People out for an evening drive. Mostly the motorcycle crowd and a few locals who come for Thursday night all-you-can-eat chili and corn bread.''

"It's early yet."

Or nine years too late, she thought. "I've got to bake a couple of pies and mix up the corn bread. You enjoy your coffee . . ." Three pairs of blue eyes looked up at her, so identical she wondered how Dean could not help but see the similarity. "And boys, you behave yourselves. Dr. Weylin might want a little peace and quiet with his coffee." She'd made a difficult personal sacrifice to make sure he'd never have one little boy—much less two—disrupting his life. *And* his career.

Chapter Two

"He's the one, isn't he?"

"Don't say a word, Pop. Not one word." With more force than intended, Sunny scooped shredded beef onto a tortilla already spread with refried beans, then drizzled grated cheddar across the top. There were dinner customers waiting for their orders, most of them looking forward to bowls of chili and corn bread. Dean Weylin was still here, too. She wished he'd go back to wherever the boys had found him.

"I'm not so senile I'd forget a face like his. Good-looking son of a—"

"It doesn't matter, Pop. He doesn't remember me."

"Not remember?" her grandfather sputtered. "Hell, he slept with you, didn't he?"

The evidence was all too obvious—Howard Dean and Daniel Harrington McCloud—twins with beautiful blue eyes. She'd been a sentimental fool to name them after their father, but then, she'd never expected to see him again. Hadn't wanted to, she'd told herself.

But that had been a lie.

Now she didn't know quite how she felt. Protective of the boys. Hurt that Dean didn't remember her. Harboring a simmering anger she refused to acknowledge. Determined to keep her distance and hope to goodness he'd become bored of the mountains soon, as he had so many years ago. Or maybe he'd simply been bored with her. At nineteen, she'd probably seemed unsophisticated compared to his prestigious family, scions in the medical world.

"If that young man had ruminated his responsibility for your boys like he should'a," Pop said pointedly, "you wouldn't be workin' your fingers to the bone trying to keep body and soul together. And we wouldn't be in debt up to our high towers."

Sunny ignored her grandfather's colorful, if inaccurate, vocabulary. "We're managing just fine, Pop. We had to have the new roof. We'll get the loan paid off."

"How 'bout them grabby doctors. Just 'cause a man has a heart attack, they don't have no call to come knocking on his wallet."

"I'm paying them off a few dollars each month and they're all being very patient. Things will work out." Barely. Only the fact that they'd had major medical coverage had saved them from the poorhouse.

Humphing, he ladled chili into a bowl. "If the dern snows don't come early this season, we could find ourselfs camping in a tent, and you knows it, girl."

"The drought's supposed to be over. If we have a good ski season—"

"If elephants had wings, I always say, you'd better duck."

Snatching a hot plate of corn bread from the microwave, Pop hefted the tray with the order of chili and soft tacos. *Dad burnit!* if he wasn't worried sick about what would happen to Sunny and them two sweet little boys if he up and died. His heart attack had been a nip-and-tuck thing. Sunny deserved better than being left up here in the mountains trying to run the roadhouse all by her own self. The twins deserved better, too.

He shoved through the swinging door into the dining room. If'n he could find a way, his granddaughter wouldn't have to spend the rest of her life as poor as a titmouse in an empty flour tin and looking after an ol' codger like him.

THE DINNER CROWD had thinned by the time Sunny had a chance to fix herself a bowl of chili and go in search of her children. With any luck, Dean Weylin would be gone, probably having lost interest in what little company the roadhouse had to offer.

Shoving through the door into the dining room, she instantly realized her fondest prayers had once again been ignored.

All the locals sat around one of the tables, sharing war stories about the San Gabriel Mountains. Quinn Petersen, the head ranger, and his wife, Mindy, were there, along with Gene Standish, who ran the local ski area. Among the group of familiar faces, Dean sat quietly sipping a beer. At his side were two little tousled-haired boys, who looked like they hadn't let him out of their sight in hours. The table was strewn with several of their treasures—an empty shell casing from a .22, Danny's smoky quartz, and an old belt buckle with a fleck of turquoise in the middle.

With a determined lift of her chin, Sunny repressed an urge to flee back into the kitchen.

"Hey, Sunny, how're you doing?" Mindy called, waving her over to the table. Never without her makeup carefully applied and her highlighted hair perfectly in place, Mindy was one of those enviable women who could eat endlessly without a single pound showing up on the scale. "Great chili tonight, hon."

"Thanks." She slid into the spot where Mindy had made room for her...right opposite Dean. Sunny would have preferred a seat on the far side of the room where she couldn't feel his eyes tracking her every movement.

"Where's Billy?" Sunny asked her friend without meeting Dean's gaze.

"He and Pop are in the other room watching a re-run of 'Gilligan's Island.'"

Sunny slid Howie and Danny a questioning look. Billy was one of their best friends and "Gilligan's Island" was one their favorite TV shows. What strange genetic pull had them latched onto Dean so tightly, when their normal behavior included the avoidance of adults?

"Don't you want to go watch, too?" she asked the boys.

"Naw, we already seen it," Howie responded.

"Dean's been telling us how he got shot." Danny was up on his knees reaching for the .22 casing. "It was a bigger bullet than this even. Right in his head. There was blood and gore everywhere!"

"What a lovely dinnertime conversation," Sunny said. Fortunately she didn't have much of an appetite anyway. At least the morbid topic explained the boys' fascination with Dean.

"They were curious." Dean spoke in a voice that was strangely intimate, as though his words were meant only for her ears. "The truth is, I don't remember much about that night at all."

Sunny did. Or rather the next morning, when she'd heard the news of the shooting on the radio. The report and the clawing emotions she'd experienced had been permanently embedded in her memory.

"Sounds to me like Dean is lucky to be alive at all," Mindy commented.

"Hey, I got shot once, and you didn't hardly give me any sympathy at all," her husband, Quinn, complained.

"You shot yourself in the foot with Billy's BB gun. If you'd have listened to me, we wouldn't have had the thing in the house in the first place."

Gene laughed at Quinn's expense. Wiry and good-humored, Gene had once been a contender for the Olympics in cross-country skiing. A slip on a rugged portion of a downhill slope had ended that ambition. "Sure glad we have you to rely on for our safety, Quinn. I'll remember that the next time there's a maverick bull moose on the loose up on the ski slopes."

"Well, it hurt," Quinn grumbled. A big man with broad shoulders and massive biceps, in a prior century he might have been a fur trapper or explorer. Marriage to a local girl had kept him closer to civilization than he probably preferred, but he appeared happy with the arrangement. "I was barefoot. Besides, we don't have any moose in these mountains."

The conversation deteriorated into good-natured teasing as Gene and Quinn sparred, trying to one-up each other with extravagant tales of derring-do.

"Boys, have you done your homework?" Sunny asked across the table.

"Aw, Mom, do we have to?" Danny asked.

"You know the rules." In the course of being stuck on the roof, she'd forgotten to remind the boys that homework was supposed to be completed before dinner.

"We don't have much," Howie said. "Mrs. Tuttle got frazzled 'cause Brett Sanger wet his pants when she didn't let him go to the john, and she didn't assign any math homework."

As nearly as Sunny could tell, Mrs. Tuttle was often frazzled by her students' antics. It appeared to be long past time for the teacher to retire. "What kind of homework do you have?"

Danny made a face. "We gotta read some dumb old story about the Pilgrims. It stinks."

"Danny," she said sternly. "I want you both to go upstairs and do your homework. Now. Then it will be time to get ready for bed."

"Aw, Mom, we wanna hear more about Dean gettin' his head blown off."

She shuddered. How could they even think about something so gruesome?

"Go on, fellas," Dean interjected. "Your mother is right. Homework comes first. I'll be around for a while. Give me a high five and I'll see you tomorrow.''

With a great show of machismo, Howie and Danny slapped hands with Dean, shouted good-night to the rest of the Thursday night chili crowd, then ran through the swinging door into the kitchen. Sunny could hear their thundering footsteps on the stairs as they went up to their room.

She resented like hell her sons' easy acceptance of Dean's order about homework when they'd fought her on the subject—as they did almost every day. Where did he get off telling her boys anything?

She fumed, but didn't say a word. He'd be gone in a couple of days. Things would get back to normal. Dean Weylin wasn't a man to stick around the mountains for long.

Tossing back the last of his beer, Dean wondered if Sunny knew how lucky she was. Granted it couldn't be easy to be a single parent of two energetic boys. But she seemed to have a lot of help and was surrounded by good friends. In contrast, he'd been so focused on his career he'd had little chance to develop relationships that went beyond family and profession.

When he woke from a week-long coma, his folks had been there. And his brother Rick. But no woman had fretted over his survival or looked at him in the same devoted way as Mindy looked at her husband.

Now, because of some gang-banger who'd gone crazy on dope, it was very likely no woman would ever find that much to admire about Dean. Because he didn't have a damn thing to offer.

He stood and stepped over the bench. "Time for me to go, too."

Quinn extended his hand. "Enjoy your stay. The campground isn't fancy, but we like to think of this part of the San Gabriels as our little piece of heaven."

"It'll do," he conceded. Sunny, he noted, didn't look up. In fact she'd studiously avoided eye contact the whole time she'd been sitting at the table. It made him wonder if she didn't want him anywhere near her small slice of paradise.

"I enjoyed the chili," he said to the top of her bent head. "Thanks."

"You're welcome."

Forced to look up, she met his gaze for the first time. A white-hot flash burst at the edges of his awareness, then vanished just as quickly, leaving a residual pain so intense it almost made him double over. He walked away before anyone could notice the sweat that dampened his face. Not since he'd woken in the hospital had he been so troubled by the electrical currents misfiring in his brain.

Acutely aware of his departing footsteps, Sunny continued to stare at the spot he had recently vacated. Before he'd been able to recover himself, she'd seen the slight tightening around his sensuous lips, the flash of pain in his eyes and the hint of a frown forming. He was still suffering from his wound, she realized. In spite of all good reason, she wished she had the right to offer him comfort.

Mindy poked her in the ribs. "Wow! Where did you find him?" she asked.

Blinking, Sunny was surprised to discover herself near tears. She swallowed them back. "Actually the boys found him."

"I've always thought your twins had the prettiest eyes for boys. This guy Dean has eyes just as gorgeous. Downright sinful to waste them on a man."

"Really? I hadn't noticed." She concentrated on swallowing a spoonful of cold chili past the tight lump in her throat.

"Didn't notice?" Mindy sputtered. "Have you gone blind?"

"I've been busy."

"A hunk like him wanders into your restaurant— great body, super nice with your kids, generally a guy to die for, and single, for heaven's sake—and you don't bother to take a second look? Girl, you've been working too hard!"

Sunny laughed. It seemed like a good way to divert her friend from probing further with questions Sunny didn't want to answer. "I promise to pay more attention if he comes in again. How's that?"

Looking at her as if she'd just grown a second head, Mindy said, "You do that, hon. Or I'm going to call in the men with the white coats and the giant-size butterfly nets. They'd know what to do with you."

Sunny figured if Dean stayed in the mountains for any length of time she would indeed go crazy. How long would it be before Mindy and everyone else noticed the strong family resemblance between the twins and the man they'd become so instantly attached to? Pop was already in on the secret. Soon others would begin developing suspicions of their own.

A wintry shiver raced down her spine. What if Dean discovered the truth and, with the backing of his powerful family, decided to claim custody of his sons?

HE'D MADE IT to page twenty in the book.

For company, he'd had the campground's resident blue jay, who'd spent the better part of the afternoon complaining that no snacks had been provided for his enjoyment. A couple of campsites away, a squirrel was busily dropping pinecones to the ground. They crashed through the tree branches, landing with a thud. The squirrel soon followed, determined to find the seeds hidden inside the cone's petals.

On the highway that rode the crest of the San Gabriels, a heavy vehicle ground its gears, shifting down to climb a steep incline. The school bus, Dean guessed.

Sitting at the picnic table, he resumed laboriously copying *Grey's Anatomy* letter by tortuous letter onto lined notebook paper, struggling to pronounce the words and make sense of them. His hand cramped and he stretched his fingers. He was determined to relearn all the skills he'd lost in the shooting.

Whatever it took.

You can bet his father, Harrington D. Weylin, Jr., Chief of Staff at University Hospital, had not intended to raise a functional illiterate. *An unemployable bum,* Dean thought bitterly as he recalled his father's harsh words when his younger brother, Rick, had dared drop out of college.

In the next month, Dean had to get his act together. That's when he was scheduled to resume his surgical rotation to finish up his residency. His father had made special arrangements to accommodate whatever limitations Dean might still be experiencing. But resume his residency, he would. Ol' dad wouldn't take no for an answer. The Weylin men, three generations worth, became surgeons at University Hospital, and then they were selected Chief of Staff. That's simply how it was done.

Looking up, Dean saw the twins coming in his direction.

"Hey, Dean!"

"What'ja doin'?"

Resting his pencil, Dean watched Howie and Danny racing across the campground. Their shirttails were hanging out, Danny had a grass stain on one knee of his denim pants, and both of them had untied shoelaces that whipped around, coming dangerously close to tripping them. Dean imagined the twins had looked far more presentable when Sunny had sent them off to school that morning.

The thought of Sunny brought a smile to his lips. He'd been tempted all day to walk up the hill for a cup of coffee. And maybe some conversation.

But last evening she hadn't seemed all that eager for his company. He figured he'd better leave well enough alone.

"How'd school go?" he asked as the boys piled onto the bench across the table from him.

Howie shrugged. "Okay, I guess."

"Mrs. Tuttle had a cow when I messed up a math problem on the blackboard. Said I was just fooling around." Danny fiddled with an acorn that had landed on the table. "You oughta see her face when she gets mad. Beet red."

Probably hypertensive, Dean automatically thought. "Maybe you ought to take it easy on her then. Teaching's not an easy job."

"You wanna help us look for gold?" Danny asked. "Billy's dad says there might be some down by the creek."

"Not today, kids." Dean picked up his pencil. "I've got work to do."

Twisting around to peer at the open book, Howie asked, "What's that?"

"It's an anatomy book. All about bones and blood vessels. Things like that." Subjects that were once second nature to Dean, and now were like a foreign language.

"Neat! Gory stuff, right?" Danny's eyes lit up mischievously. "I bet we could really gross out Becky Ragsdale with a book like that. She's so prissy."

Dean chuckled. He remembered a prissy girl in his fourth-grade class who the boys had loved to tease. Strangely he remembered a lot of details about elementary school. It was the later years that had been snatched from his memory by the stray bullet.

Howie continued his perusal of the text and Dean's painstakingly copied notes. "You writing out that whole big book?"

"That's the plan."

"How come?"

"I'm trying to learn anatomy." All over again.

"Oh." He lifted his shoulders in a disinterested shrug. "You write the same way Danny does."

Dean looked from Howie to his brother. "What do you mean?"

"You know, you mix up stuff. Like write your *b*'s backwards. Stuff like that."

"I don't do that," Danny insisted.

"Sure you do."

"Do not!"

"I've seen ya!"

"Liar!"

"Hey, boys, take it easy. You don't have to fight about it."

Danny's lower lip jutted out in a pout. "Come on! Are we gonna look for gold, or aren't we?"

The discussion came to an abrupt halt at the sound of their grandfather calling them. "Howie! Danny! Get yourselfs on home. Your mother wants you."

"Aw, gee!" they chorused.

"On your way, kids. You better do what your mother says."

With audible sighs, they trudged back across the campground, stopping briefly to talk with Pop. The kids went on their way up the hill, while the old man headed toward Dean. He guessed the boys' great-grandfather to be about eighty. Nearly bald, the top of his head sported a dozen age spots; what must have been muscle in his youth had now turned to extra weight around his middle.

"Afternoon," the old man said as he arrived at Dean's campsite. "That there vehicle of yours sure is fancy."

Dean glanced over his shoulder at his camping van with a pop-up top. "It's comfortable enough for one."

His needs weren't complex these days—a bed and a place to cook his meals were his only requirements.

"Bet it set you back a pretty penny."

"It wasn't too bad. I bought it used."

"That a fact." With something clearly on his mind other than camping, he jammed his hands into his trouser pockets. "Guess if you got enough dough to handle a rig like that, you ain't lookin' for no job."

"Job?" At this point, Dean couldn't imagine any occupation for which he was qualified.

"My granddaughter, Sunny, been working so hard she never gits a chance to rest her bones. Like when she was climbing up on the roof yesterday. It's not fittin' a girl ought to have to do work like that. Not fittin' at all."

"She seemed to be managing all right till the boys knocked over the ladder," Dean said pointedly.

"Maybe." Pop walked over to examine the inside of the van. "But still, she has to cook and scrub, dawn to dinnertime, she does. And I'm not as much help as I used to be. Fact is, I been looking to hire a helper for her. Thought maybe if you needed a little extra change rattling around in your trousers . . ."

"Not really."

"Had a couple a fellas workin' for us back a spell, but Sunny made me lay 'em off. Cost too much, she said. She only kept on our weekend help. Did that only 'cause she likes spending a little extra time with the twins when they don't have no school to go to. Thought maybe I could talk her into hiring you, what with you being right here and all, to help out some during the week."

"I don't exactly need the money." That, at least, wasn't one of his problems. A modest bequest from his grandmother a couple of years ago assured Dean that he'd never starve to death, though the funds were too limited to handle major expenses like med school.

"Figured not, what with you being able to buy a fancy outfit like this. Not your problem, anyways, her being sick and all."

"Sunny's sick?"

"She won't talk about it none. Doctor says..." He swiped his palm across the top of his head.

"What's wrong with her?"

"Well, now...fact is, if Sunny knew I'd mentioned one word to you, she'd have a fit. Proud woman, that girl. Stubborn as a horse what gets a whiff of the barn and won't change her direction till she gets there. Same way, Sunny wouldn't think of asking nobody for help. Not a soul."

"I'm not sure what I can do." If she was already seeing a doctor...

"Well now, seems to me a smart fella like you could figure how to wheedle your way into helping Sunny without her being none the wiser. You could just sorta hang around. Start with finishing stringing them lights like she was trying to do yesterday. If you just plain went about doing it, she couldn't hardly stop you, now could she?"

"I suppose not."

Admittedly Dean wasn't pleased with the thought of Sunny climbing back up that long extension ladder and risking another disaster. If she was really ill...well, it wouldn't take all that much time away from his own studying, and it would be a hell of a lot less frustrating.

"Seems to me, if'n you was hanging around when it came time to mop up at night, now that'd be a real help."

Him mop a floor? Not that he was too good for any job these days, but suddenly Dean had the distinct impression he was being conned. He didn't normally fall for a sob story. Maybe the ol' geezer had gotten to him because he'd already developed a substantial amount of interest in Sunny McCloud—a serious fascination which had nothing to do with mopping floors.

He closed the book on the picnic table and slid the loose papers beneath it so they wouldn't blow away. "Why don't I start with fixing the lights? Then we'll see how it goes from there."

Pop's grin was so wide, it looked as if he'd just won the lottery.

Chapter Three

Something banged against the front of the road-house, shaking the whole building.

Curious, Sunny set aside the canned goods she'd been putting away in the pantry and went outside. The boys were upstairs changing out of their school clothes, so they couldn't be making the racket. She hoped. On the other hand, as typical eight-year-olds, Mischief and Trouble were unpredictable.

So was Dean Weylin, she realized, failing to suppress an unwelcome flutter of pleasure at the sight of him halfway up the ladder. Among other attributes, Dean had incredible buns.

She quashed the thought almost as quickly as it arose.

"What are you doing?" she asked.

"Stringing Christmas lights."

"You don't have to do that." It would have been better if he'd stayed at the campground—or went back to L.A., for that matter. Staying as far away from her boys as possible would be her preference. "I was going to finish up that job this afternoon."

"I didn't want to have to rescue you again." Leaning away from the ladder, he stretched as far as he could to pound in a nail.

Instinctively she steadied the old ladder, which was often unstable. "I'm perfectly capable of stringing a few lights without your help."

"Maybe I just wanted another free cup of coffee."

She rolled her eyes. Dean had always been a little hard to discourage, not that she'd made much of an effort nine years ago. To her everlasting regret.

He clambered down the ladder and she stepped back. As nearly as she could tell, his injury hadn't affected his physical abilities. He was still as agile and athletic as he'd always been.

"You really don't have to do this," she said when he landed on the ground. He was still tall—so tall he made her feel both vulnerable and feminine at the same time.

Eyeing her speculatively, he moved the ladder over a few feet. "Sure I do. I was a Boy Scout. They taught me to help little old ladies cross the street and to do a good deed every day."

"Right." She bit off the word with a slash of sarcasm. "That means you're supposed to be trustworthy, loyal, helpful, brave, reverent—"

"All except the reverent part." The corner of his mouth hitched into an unnerving half smile and his gaze swept over her in blatant masculine appraisal, then settled on her lips in a warm caress that stole her oxygen away. "I'll leave that particular virtue to others."

With the arrogance of the totally self-assured, he started up the ladder again, leaving Sunny rooted to the spot, her heart clamoring so loudly she was afraid he'd be able to hear it clear up on top of the roof.

Damn him for still having the power to turn her knees rubbery with a single provocative glance! It wasn't fair. And she darn well wasn't going to give him the satisfaction of knowing how much he affected her.

He *wasn't* trustworthy. She'd given him her heart; he'd walked away without looking back. The same went for loyalty. He didn't know the meaning of the word. Dean Weylin needed a remedial course in Boy Scouts 101.

"Do what you want," she called up to him. "But if you break your neck, don't come crawling to me for sympathy."

His laughter rained down on her like sunshine dappling through pine trees on a hot summer day.

Whirling, she marched into the restaurant. She needed to work, to keep busy. That's how she'd survived nine years ago. She wouldn't take time to think. To remember. Never again would Dean Weylin reduce her to that magnificent madness she'd experienced for one brief summer... with him.

CARRYING THE LADDER back to the toolshed where Pop had told him it belonged, Dean spotted two escaping felons sneaking out the kitchen door, both of them about eight years old. By the way they were acting, he had a fair idea they hadn't been paroled by their mother.

"Hey, you guys, where're you off to?"

His question brought them to a sheepish halt. Dean stifled a laugh at the guilt that was written all over their otherwise innocent faces.

"Out," Howie said.

"That so?" Dean asked casually. He lowered the ladder against the shed that provided storage for an assortment of gardening and snow-shoveling equipment. "Where to?" He suspected it was somewhere that didn't include homework.

Danny's scowl was intended to slow even the fiercest dragon in his tracks. "We gots business. That's all."

"Uh-uh? Let's check it out with your mom."

"You're not the boss of us," Danny protested.

"Come on, Danny," Howie said in a defeated sigh. "She's gonna make us do our homework, anyways. Besides, if we get it done tonight, maybe she'll let us go up to the fire lookout tomorrow, and we can look for more smoky quartz and gun-shell casings. We haven't got that much stuff to do."

Danny didn't look convinced.

"I'll help you," Howie offered.

With the reluctance of the damned, Danny headed for the back door. Feet shuffling, he glanced back over his shoulder.

Remembering some of the stunts he and his brother had pulled, Dean followed along in their wake. A second attempt at escape wasn't out of the question.

Inside, they found Sunny working at the grill, the scent of sizzling hamburgers roiling around her. It might not have been the most modern kitchen, but there were lots of stainless-steel countertops, a stove and grill as big as Dean had ever seen and a huge refrigerator. There looked to be enough equipment in the room to prepare meals for a small army.

His respect for Sunny revved up a notch. Running even a small restaurant was a challenge. Add that to her responsibilities as a parent, and he decided she was one hell of a lady. No wonder Pop thought she needed help. Not that Dean believed that story about Sunny being sick. He remembered enough about diagnosing illnesses to recognize Sunny was in robust good health. Definitely a woman in her prime.

She turned to slip the cooked patty onto a bun and stopped in midmotion. Her rosy cheeks glistened with the heat from the stove. Cocking her head, she nailed him with a suspicious gaze.

"I finished up the Christmas lights and found these two making their escape when I was putting away the ladder," he explained.

Her eyes stayed locked on Dean's, giving him plenty of time to wonder if her pouty lips would taste succulent, like the hamburger she was serving up, or far sweeter. He suspected the latter.

As though she could read his thoughts, she licked her lips. Her chest rose in a sigh as she purposefully directed her attention away from Dean and to the twins.

"I thought you boys said you had homework."

"Not much," Howie said.

"We've got all weekend. How come we have to do it now?" Danny complained.

"Because those are the rules."

She finished putting the hamburger together, then hooked the back of her wrist at her waist, unintentionally emphasizing the sexy swell of her hips. Her breasts thrust enticingly against the front of her bib apron. Dean knew he shouldn't be thinking about how those delicate breasts would feel in his hands, how he'd like to cup them gently, and taste them when he'd finished savoring the flavor of her lips. But his surprisingly overactive libido had other ideas.

For a man who hadn't seriously looked at a woman in nine months, Sunny McCloud had certainly attracted his attention. Why her? he wondered. And why the strange feeling that the answer should be obvious?

"Get your books, boys," Sunny ordered, gesturing toward a table at the end of the kitchen that looked as if it was their usual place for studying. "And get busy."

She shifted her attention back to Dean. "Thank you for bringing the twins back inside. I'll see to it they don't bother you anymore."

"The kids aren't a bother." He tucked his fingertips into the hip pockets of his jeans. "I'm sure my brother and I got into as much mischief as Danny and Howie do.''

"Yes, well..."

Pop pushed into the kitchen through the swinging door. "We got ourselfs a passel of bikers looking for supper out there. I'm keeping up with the crowd at the bar, but I could sure use some help taking their dinner orders."

Picking up a rag to wipe her hands, Sunny said, "I'll be right there."

"No you don't, missy. You can't do the waitering and cooking all at the same time. Not with the crowd that we got now."

"We've always managed before."

He shot Dean a pointed look. "I 'spect this young fella would be glad to help us out."

Dean felt a moment of panic. "Me?"

"Sure, you. I'm offering you a job, fella. It don't pay much—"

"I can't cook."

"I'm sure Dr. Weylin has no interest in working for—"

"He can waiter, cain't he? Don't take no college degree to take orders."

"Pop, will you please stop interfering. Dean is a skilled surgeon. He doesn't—"

"How'd you know I was a surgeon?"

"I...I must have heard you tell the boys." Her cheeks colored.

Dean thought he'd only said doctor, not surgeon. Though neither category fit him at the moment, so it probably didn't matter.

"Now listen here, young fella," Pop said. "You gonna do the waitering or not?"

"How are the tips?" Dean asked, amused at the way the old man could manipulate a situation.

"Not bad, if'n you smile real purtylike."

At a bunch of guys who rode motorcycles? Dean thought he'd skip that part of the job.

"Okay, what do I do first?"

Sunny sputtered another objection.

"Get yourself a tray and pour a whole bunch of glasses of ice water," Pops instructed. "They all been studying on their menus, so you just have to take their orders."

How hard could that be? Dean decided.

"You don't have to do this," Sunny muttered one more time in protest as he hefted the tray and followed Pop out into the dining room. She didn't want Dean Weylin's help. Not now. Not ever.

At least with her grandfather's conniving, Dean was now out from underfoot and she could draw a steadying breath. He had an uncanny ability to unsettle her. His unexpected appearance at the back door with the boys in tow had shaken her more than she cared to admit. It was like those persistent fantasies that had plagued her years ago when she thought there was still hope she'd see Dean again. Dreams of a husband and children, how they could create the perfect family right out of a fifties sitcom.

A dream that never came true.

Jamming a wooden spoon into the pot of refried beans on the stove, she stirred for all she was worth. Tears hadn't helped then, and sure wouldn't now.

Dean reappeared in the kitchen and began rattling off the orders to Sunny.

"One well-done burger with double fries, a BLT—"

"Write them down on an order pad, Dean." She slapped a meat patty onto the grill. He was too big for the kitchen, too thoroughly masculine, too much of a distraction in the safe little world she'd created for herself and her sons.

"Write them down," he echoed with a frown. "Sure." He picked up an order pad from the countertop.

Eyeing the twins doing their homework, he said, "Hey, guys, want to help me out and get a share of my tips?"

"Hey, yeah," Danny answered excitedly.

"Sure," Howie agreed.

"I've got a system all figured out—"

"The boys need to do their studies," Sunny reminded them.

"This won't get in the way. In fact, it'll be a practical math exercise. Mrs. Tuttle would approve, I'm sure." He handed Howie the order pad and tossed him a menu. "I'll go out and take the orders. Then when I come back, you write them down and look up the prices on the menu. After that, you give the order to your mom. You two can take turns."

"I don't want to." Danny made a big production of returning to his homework, which he'd been so eager to ignore only minutes ago.

"Then I get your share of the tips," Howie told him.

"I don't care." Sprawling halfway across the table, Danny rested his head on his outstretched arm.

Sunny threw up her arms in dismay. What kind of a game was Dean up to now?

"Will the three of you make up your minds what you're going to do. There are people out there who are hungry." It was bad enough Dean had become an unwelcome helper in her kitchen—with Pop's traitorous encouragement. Now he was involving her boys in some kind of a wild scheme that was likely to cost her the goodwill of the bikers who made up a large part of her business during the off-season. And eroded her parental authority at the same time. "Get on with it!"

Dean tossed her a salute, then began dictating the order to Howie.

Sunny gritted her teeth. Didn't the man have anything else better to do with his time than irritate her? Surely there was some charitable function he was supposed to be attending this weekend. He and assorted sophisticated lady friends had been pictured on the society page often enough. Why didn't he simply trundle himself on home and leave her alone?

She went back to work at the grill. Burgers and fries, grilled cheese sandwiches, soft tacos and BLTs had made up a large part of her world for a good many years. Simple fare. She could handle that. A man she had once loved, however foolishly, reappearing in her life was a whole different matter.

As she worked, she intentionally ignored the exchanges between Dean and the twins. Even so, she was acutely aware of his comings and goings... and how the rich timbre of his voice burrowed under her skin.

WHEN THE EVENING RUSH was finally over, Sunny heaved a sigh of relief. Surely Dean would go back to the campground now.

Except he didn't.

He came back into the kitchen and parked himself at the table Danny and Howie had recently vacated in favor of watching a little Friday night television with Pop.

"This waitering, as your grandfather calls it, is hard work," Dean said. He stretched out his long legs and crossed one ankle over the other.

Sunny switched off the fire under the grill. "I'll have Pop pay you the usual wages out of the till."

"I don't want your money, Sunny."

"I didn't ask you for any favors." She never had. It wasn't her way.

"I know that." He spun one of the boy's schoolbooks around and glanced at it. "How well do the twins do in school?"

"Fine."

"Danny gets along okay?"

"Of course he does. Both boys are very smart." No doubt intelligence ran in their genes, particularly from their father's side of the family. In contrast, her judgment could easily be called into question. "I admit sometimes Danny has trouble paying attention. And a few times the teacher has reprimanded him for being disruptive in class." She frowned. His continuing interest in her children was quite disturbing. "Why do you ask?"

He hesitated, which was unusual for Dean. He was among the most self-assured men she'd ever met.

"I don't think Danny can read," he said. "Or write."

She stared at him incredulously. "Don't be ridiculous. I had his eyes checked two years ago, when Howie got his glasses. His vision is perfect."

"If I'm right, eyesight isn't his problem."

"You don't know what you're talking about." She turned away to scrape the grill, applying an extra amount of muscle to the task. "If there's something wrong with Danny, if he wasn't keeping up in school, I'd know, wouldn't I? I'm his mother." And for reasons better left unsaid, her son didn't have a father.

"Did you notice how Howie helped me out tonight by writing out the orders?"

"I'm aware you distracted the boys from their homework." And how she'd had to concentrate with all of her effort not to mix up the orders because Dean had been in her kitchen.

"Danny didn't want to help, even though he knew I was going to give them both my tips."

"Maybe he doesn't need any more favors from you than I do."

"Then, when they were doing their schoolwork, I noticed Howie was reading the assignment to him."

"The boys are very close to each other. Most twins are."

"Howie also answered the questions on the practice test for Danny."

"Oh, all right," she sighed. "Possibly the boys cheated, and I'll certainly speak to them about—"

"It's more than that, Sunny. Danny can't read. He and Howie have figured out together how to cope with his disability so no one has caught on. They've adapted very well."

Turning, she glowered across the room. "Who made you such an expert on parenting?"

"I'm not." He returned her look with unblinking confidence. "But I do know a helluva lot about dyslexia."

"I don't know what you're saying."

"People who can't read make adjustments in their behavior in order to cope with whatever demands are placed on them. If they can't read street signs, they memorize what's on every corner where they have to make a turn in order to get to work. Or in a restaurant, they always order the same thing, or what the guy at the next table is having, because the menu is gibberish to them."

"So?"

"Did you think it was a little odd I wanted the boys to write out the orders for me tonight?"

"Well, yes, but I thought—"

"I can't read, Sunny. At least not above a very basic level. The bullet that went into my head short-circuited that part of my brain that can make sense out of symbols. I'm functionally illiterate."

She gaped at him astounded. His brilliant mind, all those years of medical training he had coveted to the exclusion of starting a family too early. Now he couldn't even read. The realization made her sick to her stomach.

"I didn't know," she said softly.

"I didn't intend for you to. I'm not exactly proud of the situation, so I adapted as best I could to cover up. I conned Howie—an eight-year-old kid—into doing a simple task that I'm not capable of doing for myself."

She wondered what the admission of illiteracy had cost Dean in terms of his ego but was even more concerned about her son. "You think Danny's doing the same thing?"

"Based on what I've heard and seen—including an odd comment Howie made about Danny's handwriting—I think you'd be wise to have him tested. He's young enough that he should be able to improve his skills. A lot of adults are very successful even though they have difficulty reading."

Stunned, she leaned back against the work counter and closed her eyes. Images came to her of the boys doing their homework, their curly little heads close together—and Howie doing all the actual work. Time and again the clues had been there. If she'd only been paying attention.

"Oh, my God . . ." She covered her mouth with her hand, guilt rising in a wave that nearly swamped her. "I should have known. I should have seen what was happening. I'm their mother. . . ."

Dean's hands were at her shoulders, consoling her, lending his strength. She didn't have the courage to move away. For a few brief moments, she wanted the luxury of not having to face a crisis alone.

"Don't beat yourself up for not figuring out what was going on." His hands moved gently, tenderly, up and down her arms. "They're clever kids—smarter than most grown-ups, I imagine—and you're not a trained educator."

She sniffed and blinked back unwelcome tears. She wished Dean weren't being so damn nice. "I was going to be a teacher." Until she'd found herself pregnant with no one to rely on but herself and an aging grandfather.

Looking up into his face, she noted he must have shaved that morning, but now there was a slight stubble of whiskers. She wondered at the wound that had cost him the ability to read and how much that loss must have pained him. As much as the injury itself, she imagined.

As though she had no control over her actions, her fingers touched the spot just above his temple where he'd been shot. "I'm sorry about what happened to you."

"Given the circumstances, I got off easier than I might have. I may not be able to read, and I lost a big chunk of my memory, but at least I'm not a vegetable.''

"Your memory?''

"Yeah. I remember things about being a kid, but most of my adult life is gone. I only get flashes of scenes from med school. Or the year the family all went to France. That must have made a real impression on me. I can remember what a carotid artery is, but I can't remember where the hell it's supposed to be in a human body. Whole years of my life, and what I learned in them, are simply a blank.''

Slowly the implications of what he was saying seeped in. "There's a reason why you've forgotten,'' she whispered, awed. *A reason why he'd forgotten her.* A small bud of hope she didn't want to acknowledge blossomed in her chest.

"A reason, yeah. But it doesn't make the loss any less frustrating.''

It did for Sunny. If he had forgotten her, there was at least a physical reason for his memory loss. It wasn't necessarily that he hadn't cared . . .

But he hadn't cared, she reminded herself, her hopes crumbling almost as soon as they had appeared. He'd walked away from her—and the children she was going to bear—long before the shooting. The coincidence of his arrival at Cloud High Roadhouse was only that. He was recovering from a serious injury. Lots of people chose the mountains as a place to rest and rejuvenate.

She placed her palms on his unyielding chest. "I'll talk to Mrs. Tuttle, the boys' teacher, next week.''

"I'll come with you."

"I don't want you to."

"Look, from what the boys have told me, their teacher is a little past her prime. Unfortunately I'm sort of an expert on dyslexia. I can help."

"But I don't want your help."

"Your grandfather warned me you could be stubborn."

"That's not—"

She swallowed her objection as he cupped her chin and ran the pad of his thumb across her lower lip in a blatant attempt to arouse her. It worked. In spades. Her breathing accelerated. So did her heart rate. Instantly, as though she'd been programmed to respond to Dean's special touch, her whole body stirred awake.

"You're real uncomfortable with me around," he said with husky undertones that vibrated through her midsection. "I'm curious to know why."

"I'm not . . ." Her voice trembled on the lie.

"I've also been curious to know just how you'd taste." He lowered his head toward hers.

Sunny wasn't curious at all. She knew exactly the taste of Dean's lips, how they were full and curved, demanding from her a response she had never failed to give. She knew his musky male scent, an exhilarating combination of his spicy after-shave and an aroma that was specifically his own body chemistry. She'd always imagined his compellingly unique fragrance as being half stud and half intellectual giant, with a dash of arrogance thrown in.

Instinctively her fingers curled into the fabric of his shirt. A weighty warmth invaded her limbs along with a debilitating sensation of melting. Anticipation grew. This was the man who had taught her the limits of sensual delight, the lover who she had dreamed about for years after he was gone.

Gone.

The realization stiffened her spine.

Dean Weylin had no right to kiss her. Not here in her kitchen, not here in her home where she'd raised their children on her own.

"No." The word was a groan of denial against his determined lips.

Dean pulled back with a start. The sense of déjà vu was a potent thing, filled with color and tactile memories, perceived through a haze that clouded his vision. He shook his head to rid himself of the mental cobwebs. It didn't work.

Sunny's eyes had darkened until they were a deep blue, familiar somehow, yet why he would recall them remained elusive. Her lips glistened and he had the distinct feeling he had sipped their flavor before. But where? When? And if that were true, why wouldn't she have told him?

Chapter Four

"You shouldn't have done that," Sunny whispered, the words thickening in her throat. Despite the sacrifices he'd forced her to make, she'd still reacted to him, *wanted* him with the same maddening need of her youth. She hadn't grown one whit wiser or smarter in all these years. That made her mad as hell at herself. *And* him. "You had no right to kiss me."

"Something tells me I did." He framed her face between his palms, capturing her in a tender vise, his agate blue eyes filled with questions she wasn't about to answer. "Furthermore, I suspect we're going to do a lot more than kiss before this is all over."

Her pulse jumped. "You suspect wrong." It had been over for nine years. He'd never called. Never come back. How could she have expected otherwise?

"How come I make you so nervous? I'm just a guy."

"A guy who's just passing through. That ought to be reason enough."

"You get a lot of travelers on this highway?"

"None who stay long." He'd been the only one she'd allowed to linger, and that had been a serious mistake on her part.

"Your choice? Or theirs?"

"Mine."

"Then I think we've got a problem here. I'm kind of enjoying this little piece of paradise."

"*We* have a problem? *I've* got a problem because you're standing in my kitchen mauling me—"

"The mauling was mutual. You reacted, honey. I didn't dream it. Though I admit, I enjoyed it. And I have the oddest feeling that this wasn't the first—"

"Good night, Dr. Weylin." She shoved his arms aside and stepped away. Panic roiled hot in her chest at the thought he might remember the past. Worse, that he might remember and reject her and the boys all over again. "The café is closed for the night. And so is this subject."

Eyes narrowed, Dean managed to stop himself from pulling Sunny back into his arms, willing or not. Their kiss had staggered him. She was sinfully sweet, hot and wild all at once. A dynamite combination. Maybe he was only passing through, with nothing to offer Sunny but a helping hand at "waitering," but she sure as hell made him wish otherwise.

Since the shooting, he'd been faced with many journeys of rediscovery. He suspected that unraveling the truth about Sunny, and why she triggered such a powerful response in him, would be the most intriguing exploration of all.

WHILE HOWIE was still brushing his teeth in the bathroom, Sunny took the opportunity to sit down on the edge of Danny's bed to have a little heart-to-heart.

He grinned up at her. "You look tired, Mom."

"It was a long day." He was the more sensitive of her two sons, the one most likely to bring home an injured bird to nurture, or notice when she was particularly weary. She cherished these quiet bedtime moments with her boys, a chance to reconnect after a hectic day.

"Tell me, Danny, how are you getting along in school?"

He wrinkled his nose. "Okay, I guess."

"Just okay?" Brushing back a wayward curl from his forehead, she marveled at how closely his hair resembled his father's in texture, if not in color. She wondered if Dean had been a towhead when he was young and regretted that there were so many details of his life he'd never shared with her. They'd been so wrapped up in old-fashioned lust, she supposed, there hadn't been much time for getting to know each other.

"School's boring." He squirmed and flopped over onto his side. "I don't know why I have to learn all that stuff anyways."

"So you can make a decent living when you grow up."

"I'm gonna find gold, Mom. Billy's dad says there's lots still around."

"I'm not so sure. It takes a lot of work and know-how to find gold these days."

"Or maybe I'll be a professional baseball player and make a million bucks playing for the Dodgers. I don't need to learn all that stuff in school."

"Honey, if you're having trouble, we can get you help. I don't want you to fall too far behind—"

"Jeez, Mom, do we have to talk about school all the time?"

Danny's avoidance of the subject lent credence to the suggestion that there might be something wrong. It hurt like crazy that it had taken Dean less than twenty-four hours to detect Danny's problem, when she'd been totally oblivious.

Reappearing from the bathroom, Howie climbed into the adjacent twin bed and placed his glasses on the nightstand. Their bedroom reflected two different sets of interests: Dodger baseball pennants decorating the wall above Danny's bed, and pictures of dinosaurs and astronauts festooning Howie's half of the room. There was a distinct difference in the relative neatness of each side of the room, too. She'd never been able to convince Danny that being tidy was a worthwhile attribute. He was simply too disorganized to live with anything but clutter.

"I'm sick of hearing about what Billy's dad says and does," Howie grumbled. "He's not so great."

Frowning, Sunny said, "Quinn is a very nice man. You boys have always liked him."

"Yeah, but Billy's always bragging about him…like his dad is so perfect. The only reason he says stuff like that is 'cause he knows we don't have a dad. He's just being a jerk."

Pain knotted in her chest. They *did* have a father, but one who'd been so determined to pursue his career, she hadn't been willing to impose unplanned parenthood on him, too. Not that she'd believed he would have been interested. Far from it.

"Hey, Mom?" Danny questioned. "Did our father not stick around 'cause Howie and me are weird, or something?"

"Oh, no, sweetheart. You boys had nothing to do with what happened." At least not beyond the fact they'd been conceived at the time. "I've told you, he was a very busy, important man. If anyone's at fault that you don't have a father around, it's me." She'd made the ultimate decision, the *right* decision. Without even asking, she'd known darn well it was the decision Dean would have wanted.

"Did you do something wrong, Mom?"

In a careless moment, she'd fallen in love and then had to sacrifice that love on the altar of the career Dean had chosen. "Not wrong, exactly. But I did do something that you could say was foolish." She gave Danny's nose a teasing tap with her fingertip. "But I was lucky, 'cause I ended up with you two guys."

"Hey, I know what we can do," Howie announced. He had that mischievous twinkle in his eyes that usually meant trouble. "We can find Mom a man to marry and then we'd have a dad."

"Let's find somebody who's rich," Danny chimed in.

"Now wait a minute—"

"Somebody like Einstein. You know, a smart guy who knows all about chemistry and stuff so we can make cherry bombs 'n stuff."

"I want a dad who's a baseball player. A pitcher like—"

"Boys! That's enough." Torn between laughter and tears, she tucked Danny's blankets up around his chin and gave him a kiss. She was hurting and the boys weren't making things easy for her tonight. "We have Pop and he's the only man we need."

"He's old," they chorused.

"He loves you both. That's what counts." She tucked Howie in, too, the love she felt for him and his brother filling her chest until she thought she would burst. It should be enough. "Behave yourself, young man. There'll be no matchmaking in this house, thank you very much."

His smile creased his cheeks—a devastatingly close replica of his father's wicked grin. "Does that mean you'll get me a chemistry set of my own for Christmas?"

"If I do, you can bet there won't be any chemicals in it that could make a bomb."

"Not even a small one?"

She kissed him good-night. "Not even."

"Is it okay if we go up to the fire lookout tomorrow?" he asked in an easy shift of topic.

"I suppose. How 'bout the three of us make a day of it? I'll make us a picnic." She liked to indulge herself on the weekends by spending time with the boys, even though it cost extra to hire help to staff the roadhouse. Soon enough the twins would be teenagers and have no interest in hanging around with their mom at all. And tomorrow a picnic would provide a perfect excuse to avoid seeing Dean.

"Yeah, neat," Danny agreed. "Maybe we can find some more bullets and stuff."

"Or snakes," Howie added.

She shuddered at the thought. This was definitely a case of boys having to be boys. "Good night, you two. Sweet dreams."

Her hand was resting on the light switch when Danny said, "Hey, Mom, if you married someone rich you wouldn't have to work so hard, would you?"

"I don't know, honey. I've never been rich."

She turned off the light, stepped into the hallway and closed the door behind her. A silent sob ripped through her chest. Why did Dean have to reappear in her life making her want things she couldn't have? For herself. For her boys. It simply wasn't fair.

Blinking back her tears, she tried to subdue the irrational longing that tugged at her heart.

At the end of the hall the light in Pop's room glowed under his door. She wished she could talk to him, but he hadn't understood nine years ago why she'd had her babies alone. Or why her mother had made the same decision years ago. She didn't imagine he'd understand any better now.

She turned down the hallway toward her own room. A car hummed by on the highway and a night bird called in the lonely silence that followed. A floorboard creaked where she stepped, a forlorn, solitary sound. She'd never felt more alone, more needy than she did at this very minute.

Dammit! He shouldn't have kissed her. She'd tried so hard to forget.

Once in her bedroom, she took off her work clothes and pulled her short nightgown over her head. Her skin seemed particularly sensitive as the brushed cotton caressed her flesh, sliding down across to her breasts, making her nipples pucker. The memory of Dean's kiss lingered, the texture of his tongue as he claimed her mouth after so long an absence. His masculine scent a powerful aphrodisiac.

Standing in front of the pine dresser that had once been her mother's, Sunny loosened the braid and tugged her fingers through her hair. Tilting her head, she began to brush her hair in rhythmic strokes. Once, after they had made love, Dean had done this for her, his strokes strong yet gentle, his breath warm across the back of her neck.

Her chin trembled.

She couldn't think about the past. He'd be gone in a few days. Not for a minute did she expect him to hang around long in her mountains.

But, dear God, her boys needed a father.

If there was any chance Dean would want to be a part of their lives, did she have a right to keep them apart?

Or was the risk too great he would come between her and her sons if he knew the truth?

Haunted by memories she'd tried to repress, she knelt and opened the bottom drawer of the dresser.

Beneath her sweaters, secreted inside her high-school yearbook, she found the one snapshot she had of Dean and herself. A grandmotherly tourist had taken the photo and sent it to her by way of thanks for their help with a flat tire. A thoughtful gesture.

Dean's smile was big and broad, his face more youthful than she remembered. The summer sun had streaked his brown hair with gold. On vacation, he'd stayed away from the barbershop longer than usual and the curls at his nape nearly touched his collar.

He was aging well, she realized. New lines at the corners of his eyes and those that had deepened around his mouth added a touch of character that had only been hinted at years ago.

Setting the photo aside, her fingers trembled as she picked up the newspaper clipping that reported the gang-related shooting in the emergency room of University Hospital. Dr. Weylin, a resident, had been hit by a random shot and was in critical condition. Sunny had called every day for a week until his condition had been upgraded to satisfactory. Only then had she been able to sleep nights.

There were other newspaper clippings, two of them. Each featured a photo of Dean as the sophisticated bachelor-about-town dressed in a tuxedo, a beautiful socialite on his arm, attending a charity function. Not exactly the typical dinner attire worn by patrons of the Cloud High Roadhouse.

She exhaled a tremulous sigh. How could she possibly trust her heart and her twins to a man who had walked away without ever looking back?

IN THE TWINS' ROOM, a night-light stuck in an outlet next to the door glowed orange. Wakeful, Danny stared wide-eyed at the shadowed shape of the chest of drawers he shared with his brother.

"Hey, Howie, you still awake?"

Blankets shifted noisily. "Yeah, I guess."

"How'd it be if we had a dad who was a doctor?"

"Huh? I thought you wanted a dad who played baseball."

Danny shrugged and scrunched his pillow into a tight ball. "If we had a dad who was a doctor, and Pop got sick again, it wouldn't cost Mom so much money to get him fixed."

Howie mumbled a response. Danny wasn't sure whether his brother agreed or not, but figured the idea of finding a father was a pretty good one. Somebody who could help take care of Mom, too.

He slipped out of bed and tiptoed to the door. Opening it as quietly as he could, he stepped into the hallway. Pop's light was still on. Danny figured with his grandfather's help they could find a way to get Dean to stick around and maybe marry his mom.

Danny stopped a moment and frowned. The only trouble was, Dean would probably nag him about doing his homework just as much as his mom. He didn't like that much but he guessed he could live with it.

DEAN HADN'T EXPECTED to learn more about Sunny by examining her underwear.

He'd come up the hill from the campground to the back of the roadhouse and there she was, hanging out the Saturday morning wash, including a whole line of lacy undies in reds and blacks and floral prints. In spite of knowing it was an intrusion on a woman's privacy, he fingered the sheer material. Silk, soft and sensuous. Bikini style, the legs were cut high, the wisp of fabric barely big enough to shield a woman's most alluring secrets. He could picture her in them—the soft swell of her hips, a slender waist. Flesh so satiny smooth, his fingers ached with the need to caress her. His groin muscles tightened.

"Is there something you want?"

At the brusque, businesslike sound of Sunny's voice, he snatched his hand back like a kid caught with his fingers in the cookie jar. And a very nice cookie jar it was, he mused, eyeing her with heightened interest. Beneath her denim shorts she'd be wearing red lace, he imagined. Or maybe something with tiny violets that carried a sweet floral scent, like her hair. Either way, he definitely liked her style.

"Yeah." He dragged out the word.

"If you go around front, there's coffee—"

"The twins came down to the campground and told me to get on my horse. We're going on a picnic."

Her eyes widened. "They invited you?"

"You don't exactly sound happy about it."

"I'm not." She pinned a pair of kid-size jeans to the line with enough force to make the rope dip precariously.

He grinned. He liked a woman with spirit. When she got upset, she lifted her chin, and that set her long hair swaying, the length of it catching sunbeams that made it shine. "They gave me a story about there being mountain lions around and *you* needed a man to protect you."

"Me? I've lived up here all my life and never yet been attacked by a mountain lion."

"But there are lions around. I heard about an attack in the hills above Altadena a year or so ago."

"That was some kid on a mountain bike. Lions are so nearsighted, it probably thought the biker was a deer."

"Well, then, if you don't need my protection, maybe you can help me out. I can't remember ever going on a picnic, not once in my whole entire life. For all practical purposes, I'm a picnic virgin. That doesn't seem right for a guy my age."

In spite of herself, Sunny's lips twitched with the threat of a smile. She had trouble thinking of Dean Weylin as a *virgin* anything. A wealthy man-about-town, at twenty-three he'd been older and far more experienced than she during that marvelous summer of madness.

She eyed him suspiciously. "You've never been on a picnic?" She knew better and wondered if the memory had really escaped him. On more than one occasion that summer they had sneaked off into the hills to find a secluded spot. Not that food had been very much on their minds, of course. Theirs had been a different kind of a hunger.

"I didn't say I'd never been on one. I just can't remember. I do know my folks were always too busy at the country club to think about packing a lunch. Dad's idea of roughing it is slicing a shot into the trees on a golf course, and Mother thinks she's roughing it when she leaves Beverly Hills."

"Different strokes—"

"For different folks." He finished the sentence for her, completing her thought as though their minds were as much in sync today as they had been years ago. Or so she'd thought at the time.

"So can I tag along?" he asked.

She was going to dream up some new excuse to tell him no, but the twins came tumbling out of the house, shouting at full volume.

"We made the sandwiches, Mom!" Danny announced.

"Bologna and cheese."

"And peanut butter and jelly. Real gooey."

"What kind do you want, Dean?"

Their eyes were filled with so much hero worship, it caught Sunny off guard and her heart ached for them. They so desperately wanted a father, they were recruiting one of their own.

"Gee, kids, that's a hard question to answer. How 'bout one of each?"

"Yeah, great! We got chips 'n Cokes 'n some of Mom's pie, too."

"A meal fit for a king," Dean agreed.

"Pop helped us fix the stuff. But he's not coming. Says somebody's gots to watch the store."

Sunny had the distinct feeling she'd been outnumbered and outflanked by the men in her life. All of whom she loved to distraction. Except Dean, of course. She'd put that love behind her. Hadn't she?

THIS IS HOW it should have been from the beginning. Two little boys and their father roughhousing and playing king of the mountain on the granite boulders next to the abandoned fire lookout.

Sunny wrapped her arms around her knees. Wave after wave of forested hillsides rolled down toward the haze of the city as the childish laughter tumbled around her. She blinked back the hot press of tears. On a clear day, you could see all the way to the Pacific Ocean and Catalina Island. But not today.

"Those two kids have more energy than anybody has a right." Breathing hard, Dean dropped down beside her. His forehead glistened with sweat. "Maybe you ought to consider not feeding them so many vitamins."

"I've tried. Nothing seems to slow them down."

He leaned against the boulder they shared for a backrest, his lips tightening in a wince as though he was experiencing some discomfort. He drew another deep breath. He was sitting too close, so close she could see the squint lines at the corners of his eyes and the spiky golden brown lashes that framed eyes far brighter than the sky.

"Does your injury still bother you?" she asked, concerned in spite of herself.

"Not so much that." He ran his fingers through his damp hair, the curls springing back almost before he released them. "I was in the hospital for nearly a month and then had to go to rehab. Guess I haven't gotten all of my strength back yet."

Her chest tightened at the thought of how much he had suffered. She wondered who had held his hand, or soothed his pain, and wished she could have been the one. A futile desire, she admitted, but one that welled up unbidden in her chest.

He pulled a canned drink from the picnic day pack and popped the top. Tipping back the can, he took a long swig. She wanted to feel his pulse, there on his corded neck, and wondered if it matched the heavy throb of her own.

Exhaling deeply, he rested an arm on his upraised knee. His faded jeans gloved muscular thighs in fabric so soft it molded to his skin; a white T-shirt pulled tautly across broad shoulders.

Casually he reached toward her to toy with the tips of her hair where it hung straight down to the middle of her back. "I like you with your hair down."

Goose bumps tracked down her spine. "I wear it in a braid when I cook—health department rules—so when I'm not working I like to give it a rest."

"Very nice. The way the sun catches it, there must be a hundred different shades of blond in your hair." Fingering the strands, he examined them as though suddenly fascinated by each individual color.

Tilting her head, she slid her hair to the front of her shoulder. Away from Dean, away from his intimate touch.

"I don't suppose it's any of my business, but where is the boys' dad?"

Sunny tensed, her stomach knotting on the question she wanted to avoid. Automatically she glanced over her shoulder to see where the twins were. "He's not a part of the picture and never has been."

"Why not?"

A dozen reasons, most of them hard to articulate, and all based on conversations she and Dean had exchanged years ago. "He wasn't the kind of a man who had the time or interest to be a father."

"He's missing a lot."

"Yes, he is." She studied him as he watched the boys clambering over the rocks. Cautiously she asked, "Have you ever had any interest in being a father?"

"Me? Not so far." He laughed, a mirthless sound. "My specialty is—or was—surgery. Based on what little recollection I have, I spent twenty or more hours a day at the hospital as a resident, and the rest of the time I was trying to catch some sleep so I wouldn't collapse in the middle of an operation. Trust me, up till now I would have been a father in name only.''

''And now?'' Her heart thundered in her chest, slamming against her ribs. ''Since the accident? Have things changed any?''

''Yeah.'' He took another big gulp of cola. ''I'm unemployed and can barely read the label on a soup can. That hardly makes me the ideal prospect for father of the year.''

He hadn't changed, she realized. He still didn't want children in his life. The excuse sounded a little different than the one he'd given years ago, about the importance of his career and his need to succeed, but not the underlying thought.

Dean's fingers closed more tightly around the soda can. He'd given it to her straight. While he liked her kids a lot—and certainly wanted to explore a more intimate relationship with Sunny—he didn't want to mislead her into thinking he was looking to become an instant dad.

The fact was, the Weylin men—at least those who had gone into the medical profession—weren't well suited to be either fathers or husbands. The career, as they clawed their way to Chief of Staff, was too demanding, the hours too long. In the case of Dean's mother, she'd seemed happy enough with the status and financial security her husband's job had provided. Dean wasn't sure he wanted a woman like that, someone more interested in playing golf and lunching at the country club than in the welfare of her own kids.

He slanted Sunny a look. The reflection of her red T-shirt colored her cheeks with warmth; her denim shorts revealed long, shapely legs that were lightly tanned. Beneath those shorts he imagined soft, satiny silk.

Every bit of lust he'd ever read or thought about slammed into his gut. But it was more than that. The ache began to swell in a different way, somewhere in his chest. A pain that had him longing for a much deeper relationship, something with substance, a feeling that was almost tactile with its warmth and velvety texture. A strangely familiar sensation, its name escaping him on the whispering breath of a westerly wind.

Why the hell did Sunny affect him that way? It didn't make any sense at all unless—

"Smile for me, Sunny. You always look so serious, and I keep having the feeling that if you'd loosen up a bit—"

"Running a restaurant and being a single mom doesn't leave me much time for fun and games."

"But you used to laugh a lot, didn't you?" Like an echo from the past, he could almost hear the lyrical melody of her laughter. Did being a single mother mean she'd had all chance for happiness surgically removed? That was even more sad than to wake up to discover a bullet had entered your brain.

"Yes, I suppose I used to laugh more than I do now." A wistfulness appeared in her eyes, as though she were remembering dreams that had never quite been fulfilled. "I love my boys. They are my whole life. But there are days when I wish—"

The crack of a rifle shot rent the air. Instantly dirt exploded in a hail of pebbles between Dean and Sunny. Her eyes went wide.

Before Dean could react, another report echoed through the canyons. Sunny screamed.

He lunged for her. Instinctively. Without thought of the terror that whipped through his gut. The memories. The horror of a night only months ago.

His arm snaked around her middle and he dragged her behind the boulder they'd been leaning against.

"The twins," she sobbed.

"Danny! Howie! Get down."

"What's going on?" one of the boys cried.

Another shot rifled past the fire lookout. A big chunk of a pine tree splintered into the air. Panic threatened at the edges of Dean's awareness. Echoes of screams.

"On your bellies," Dean ordered the twins. Images sprang into his mind and shattered before they were fully formed. Only fear remained like a burning coal in his gut.

"Stay down!" The boys were behind the building, out of the line of fire, as far as Dean could tell. He was sweating and his adrenaline was pumping as it had that night when he'd been shot.

Dear God, he remembered! He remembered the kid coming in the door to the examining room. The gun in his hand. Big and black and lethal. Dean bending over his patient. The flash of gunpowder. Screams. People running. The pain. It throbbed at his temple like a white-hot poker. Bile rose in his throat.

"My babies," Sunny sobbed. She trembled against him. "Who's doing this? Why?" she asked hysterically. "I've got to get to my boys. We've got to get them out of here!"

She wrenched herself away from his grasp and he discovered his hand was covered in bright red blood. Her blood.

"Sunny!"

He scrambled after her, but she was quick in spite of her wound. Behind the lookout, she gathered the twins into her arms. She squeezed her eyes shut, in both pain and terror, he suspected, and Dean knew he'd never seen a woman more driven by the love for her children. Another woman might have fainted at the sight of her own blood staining her shirtsleeve. But not Sunny. She was too tough, too loving to give in to a little thing like a bullet wound. Not where her children were concerned.

"Mom! Look! They shot a bird!"

Danny darted toward the fallen blue jay, but Dean snared him by the arm. "Get down, son."

Sunny's heart leaped into her throat, fear trembling through her. "Do what Dean tells you."

"The bird's still alive, Mom. We can't just leave him there."

"You stay put," Dean ordered. "I'll get him."

"No, Dean, you don't have to—"

But it was too late. He was already half sliding and half crawling across the rocky ground to the bird. He yanked off his shirt. With infinite care, he lifted the bird. The poor thing flapped its wings uselessly, one of them bent at an awkward angle. Dean wrapped the T-shirt around the bird so only a bit of tail feathers could be seen.

Still crouched, he scuttled back to Sunny and the boys.

"You should have left the bird," she told him.

"I couldn't risk Danny getting in the way of another stray bullet. I figured I was safe enough if I stayed behind the rise of the hill." He turned to the boy. "You carry him real careful. He's scared and could hurt himself."

Danny took the bird as if it was the most precious package in the world. "I'll be careful, mister."

"That's good, son. We'll see when we get back to the roadhouse if we can fix him up. And your mom, too."

Tears burned in Sunny's eyes. Dean's *son*. A boy who had all the makings of a doctor, just like his father. Except he couldn't read.

"Hey, Mom—" Frowning, Howie cocked his head to look at her. "Is that . . . blood? On your arm?"

Feeling shell-shocked, she checked her bloody sleeve. "It's nothing, honey," she lied, suddenly feeling the sting of her wound. "Just a scratch."

"Wow! Is there a bullet in there?" Howie's expression was a confusion of fear and boyish fascination with the sight of blood. "Are you gonna die?"

"No, honey. I'm okay."

"Come on, boys," Dean urged. "Let's get your mom back home."

Chapter Five

"You should see a doctor."

"*You're* a doctor," Sunny said pointedly.

"*Was*. All I'm doing here is a little first aid."

"Your instincts are still good." His touch was incredibly gentle as he washed and applied antiseptic to the wound on her upper arm. Though it had bled profusely, it wasn't deep, a ricochet rather than a direct hit. It stung like crazy, however. She winced as he brought the edges of the jagged tear together to apply a butterfly bandage.

They'd returned to the roadhouse the back way, staying off the main trail and under cover of the forested slopes. Though there hadn't been any sign of a nut with a rifle, the hair at Sunny's nape had stayed upright the whole time. She'd kept herself between her boys and where she thought the sniper had been.

She'd only felt safe once they were all back inside the roadhouse and they'd called Quinn Petersen, the ranger, and gotten his promise to pass the word on to the sheriff's office.

She'd felt safe from the sniper, but definitely not from Dean's tender ministrations, so carefully applied in the upstairs bathroom with her sitting on the closed lid of the toilet. The room was small, too small, for a man as big as Dean. He filled the space, the overhead lighting casting intriguing shadows across his face, emphasizing his strong jaw and the deep color of his eyes.

Heat coiled low in her body at his nearness. Longing simmered in the vicinity of her heart. She wanted to throw herself into his arms and feel his masculine strength wrap around her, feel his hard velvet length filling her. She wanted comfort for both her body and soul, yet she had no right to ask. Her foolish craving threatened to engulf her and snatch her good reason away like an avalanche tearing the trees from a hillside.

Once, a long time ago, she'd given up this man so he could become a skilled surgeon. In spite of his injury, he still had the innate talent for the job. And the drive to regain his lost knowledge.

"You could use a tetanus shot," he said. "It looks like you just caught a ricochet, but stitches might be in order, too."

She sighed a shuddering breath. "I'm fine. Really."

"Isn't there a hospital down the hill in La Canada?"

"Emergency rooms cost money, Dr. Weylin. Or didn't they teach you that in med school?"

"I don't know. I can't remember." A flash of grief and residual pain appeared briefly in his eyes as an acknowledgment that he'd lost a piece of his life.

"I'm sorry," she whispered. Her fingers ached to soothe away his torment as skillfully as he ministered to her medical needs.

He studied her a moment, his gaze sweeping across her face in a penetrating perusal that brought a flush to her cheeks. "I don't mean to embarrass you," he said softly, "and I'm not saying I'm hugely wealthy, but I do have plenty of money. How 'bout I pay for you to visit a real doctor?"

Her spine stiffened. "No." She'd never taken anything from Dean. She wasn't about to start now. She'd managed alone all these years and there was no reason to change the rules at this late date. "It's only a scratch. Really."

"And I suppose if you'd fallen off the roof the other day and broken something, you would have set the bone yourself?"

"If I could. I don't like to waste my money."

"Honey, you're hell on a doctor's ego. We like to think we're worth every penny we charge." He began wrapping a gauze strip around her arm.

"Fortunately, you just told me you were no longer a doctor so I doubt I've seriously damaged your ego."

"You're quick, sweetheart. Really quick."

He laughed, a warm, full-chested sound that reminded Sunny of lazy summer afternoons, a sun high in the sky and her heart tumbling into love. She closed her eyes against the memories that assailed her. Dean smiling down at her as he entered her, filling her in ways that she hadn't known possible. His eyes darkening with passion and the swaggering, confident grin that announced she belonged to him alone. Their unspoken agreement. The incredible burst of pleasure he drew from deep within her soul.

A groan escaped her lips.

"I'm sorry. Did I hurt you?"

Oh, yes. The pain had been almost unbearable when he hadn't returned to the mountains after she'd broached, however obtusely, the subject of children and a family. He hadn't even called. He'd *known,* dammit, what she'd been trying to tell him. A man as sensitive, as caring as Dean Weylin couldn't have missed the message. Unless he'd wanted to.

She'd known then she couldn't compete with his important career, so she'd let her dream slide away.

Dean tied off the gauze strip, intentionally letting the back of his fingers linger against the softness of Sunny's flesh. Warm satin. Familiar, yet elusive, like the woman herself.

She hadn't allowed him to take off her T-shirt in order to gain access to her wound. Instead she'd rolled up her bloody sleeve, as if him seeing her in a bra would be all that terrible. Hell, he was a professional, wasn't he? Or at least he used to be.

But Sunny had a strange way of unsettling him. He wondered why.

Two pairs of thundering tennis shoes came running down the hallway.

"Dean, you gotta help the bird," Danny pleaded. "She's shaking like crazy and she won't let me get ahold of her to fix her wing."

"I'm not a vet, son. I don't know all that much about fixing—"

"But ya gotta try!"

He met Sunny's eyes with a question. The answer was obvious. He had to give it a try. And hope the kids wouldn't hate him if he failed.

"Aren't you through with Mom yet?"

Dean didn't think so. "She's all bandaged, if that's what you're asking."

"So give Mom a kiss to make her shoulder better, then come on!" Danny pleaded.

Sunny's head jerked up. "That won't be necessary."

"Maybe the kid has the right idea." Danny's suggestion certainly held a lot of appeal for Dean.

"No. You go with..."

He lowered his head, effectively silencing her. Her eyes widened. A little kiss on her shoulder sounded like a reasonable idea. Just a peck. And that's what Dean intended to do, until he veered off course at the last moment, drawn by the tip of her tongue when it darted out to moisten the fullness of her lips. What guy in his right mind could resist an invitation like that?

Danny complained loudly about the slow response to the emergency in the temporary aviary hospital set up in the kitchen downstairs, but Dean couldn't make out the words.

Sunny's irises had become a metallic blue, her breath sweet and hesitant across his face. His blood pulsed heavily through his body.

When their lips connected, he felt a jolt of high voltage electricity, as if he'd made contact with a power line. The surge whipped through him and he wanted to pull her into his arms, feel her soft body molded against his.

He hadn't realized how scared he'd been for her safety when she'd been shot. Or how much he needed now to reassure himself in every way possible that she had survived intact.

And her kid was standing three feet away nagging him about an injured bird.

Life was definitely not fair.

He broke the quick, hot kiss on a silent curse, swearing to himself he'd pursue this particular activity as soon as possible under more private conditions.

Sunny stared slack jawed at Dean's departing figure, her heart pounding an erratic beat. Blood loss had made her weak willed. That's what had happened. Otherwise she certainly would have stopped Dean from kissing her.

Next time she would.

Standing, she discovered her knees were weak and rubbery. A mild case of shock would account for that, she assured herself.

In her bedroom, she changed out of her bloody shirt, found a blouse to put on and went in search of the boys. Dean's relationship with the twins was becoming dangerously close. She didn't want the children to be hurt when Dean went back to his other life. And she was sure he would. In time, his memory would return, or at least his medical skills, and the draw of his career would pull him away.

She headed downstairs. At midafternoon, the roadhouse was relatively quiet. The weekend help was in the dining room taking a well-deserved break. She found the boys and Dean in the kitchen.

She came to an abrupt halt and a band tightened around her chest at the sight of her teary-eyed son clasping the stricken bird in his hands. Dean knelt next to the boy, stroking his hair and wiping away the tears that streaked his cheeks.

"All doctors lose patients, son. We do the very best we can, but it's not always enough."

"It's not your fault," Howie assured his brother, lifting one of the bird's wings to examine it more carefully. "She was probably old anyways."

"But she shouldn't have died." Danny's chin trembled. Bravely he tried not to give in to the emotion that threatened even greater tears. "It was only a broken wing."

Sunny's heart ached for her son.

"Maybe there was internal damage we couldn't see," Dean suggested with gentle understanding. "At least we know we did the very best we could. You can be proud of that."

Danny sniffled. "I guess."

Placing her hand on Danny's shoulder, Sunny said, "I think I've got an old shoe box upstairs. If you'd like, we can bury the bird in the box out in back. Maybe under a nice tree.''

''Birds like trees,'' Danny agreed, his voice as wobbly as his chin.

''I can dig the hole,'' Howie offered.

The funeral became a major family event. Or at least that's how Sunny thought of it.

While Howie struggled to dig a grave in the rocky soil, Danny carefully lined and covered the shoe box with aluminum foil.

Pop sat down next to Danny at the kitchen table. ''You gonna write somethin' on top of the box?'' he asked.

Thoughtfully Danny chewed on the end of a stubby pencil. ''I want to, but I always mess things up at school.''

''We'll do it together then, Danny boy. We'll make the bird real proud, we will.''

With Pop's careful guidance, Danny laboriously engraved the word ''Bird'' across the top of the aluminum-covered shoe box. Sunny turned away. It hurt too much to realize how difficult that simple writing task was for her son.

Her gaze collided with Dean across the room. He'd been watching the heart-wrenching scene, and there was as much pain in his eyes as there was in her heart, almost as if he knew he was Danny's father. But he couldn't know that, she told herself. And if he did, she wasn't at all sure he'd want to acknowledge paternity. That would be the hardest blow of all.

A few minutes later, they stood around the base of a pine tree while Danny carefully lowered the box into the hole. As naturally as if he'd always been there in difficult moments, lending his support and love, Dean linked his fingers through hers. Tears blurring her vision, she didn't have the heart to pull away.

Heat flooded her fingers and worked its way up her arm. This mindless need for Dean, the drugging desire for him had to stop. Kisses didn't mean commitment. But it would be easy to forget that—to forget the past, and repeat an old mistake. Only a fool got burned twice by the same candle.

With an aching sense of loss, Sunny withdrew her hand.

"Mom, you think the bird's flying around up in heaven now?" Danny asked.

She linked her arm around his shoulder and tugged him closer to her. Emotion crowded into her chest. "I hope so, honey. I hope so."

"YOU'RE HOVERING, you know." With a sigh, Sunny watched Dean slide into the passenger seat of her car. The boys had already scrambled into the back, delighted for a chance to avoid the stomach-jarring, hour-long ride in the school bus.

Dean's lips kicked up into a wicked grin. "Does that mean I'm wearing your resistance down?"

"Don't count on it. It's just that for the past four days, ever since some crackpot took a shot at us, you've hardly let me out of your sight." He'd even brought his books up to the roadhouse to study when he wasn't helping out by waiting tables or washing dishes. She'd expected by now he would have been long gone—had eagerly hoped he would be. "It's beginning to bug me."

"Just bein' neighborly," he assured her in a twang reminiscent of Pop.

"I don't imagine anyone's going to be taking potshots at us as we drive down the highway."

"You never know. If Quinn or the sheriff had come up with the culprit, maybe we could relax. But you heard them. They did a perfunctory search and decided the shots could have come from anywhere."

Danny leaned forward between the two front seats. "I still don't know why you want to see Mrs. Tuttle, Mom. Old Prune Face doesn't—"

"That'll be enough, Daniel McCloud. Sit back and put your seat belt on. Now."

She pulled the car out onto the highway and headed down the hill. The early-morning sun had yet to touch the pines. The air was pleasantly cool. Inside the closed car, she caught the spicy scent of Dean's aftershave. Today he was wearing a striped sport shirt that tugged across his broad shoulders; his beige slacks were casual yet elegant, his Italian loafers expensive. Simply sitting there relaxed, his elbow on the windowsill, he exuded a powerful sexuality, a sensual assault on Sunny's good reason.

She squirmed a little uncomfortably as she took a turn too fast. It was definitely too early in the morning to be aroused by the presence of a man in such close confines.

By the time they'd gone ten miles or so, they'd joined a line of fast-moving commuter cars using the mountainous shortcut from Palmdale into Los Angeles. Dean and the twins chatted amiably. Sunny concentrated on her driving. Misjudging any one of these curves could be deadly, particularly if there was oncoming traffic—as her mother had discovered nearly fifteen years ago.

Sunny rounded a curve and had to brake quickly. The cars had slowed to rubberneck at emergency vehicles parked on the opposite side of the road. A helicopter hovered twenty feet away from the side of the cliff.

"Wow! Whata ya think happened?" Howie asked.

Shuddering, Sunny said, "Looks like someone went off the road."

"Can we stop and watch, Mom? Can we? Maybe they'll bring up a body or something."

She shot a look into the rearview mirror. "Howie McCloud, you've got a terrible gruesome streak in you. Somebody may have died there. We don't need to turn it into a circus."

"Ah, gee, Mom, I didn't mean anything. It'd just be something to tell the other kids."

"I know, honey." She let him off the disciplinary hook with a half smile.

As they crept by the scene, she noted Dean craning to get a look just like the twins.

"You get many accidents along this road?" he asked.

"A fair number. People can't seem to remember to slow down."

"It's a long way to the nearest emergency room."

"Sometimes it's so far the patient doesn't make it." Sunny pulled her lip between her teeth. Her mother hadn't reached the hospital in time after her terrible accident. She'd been dead at the scene. Sunny and Pop had been left on their own.

ONCE PAST THE ACCIDENT, the cars resumed their usual commuter speed. Minutes later, the road merged with the outskirts of La Canada. The hustle and bustle of heavy traffic and flashing signal lights was in sharp contrast to the more peaceful pace up in the mountains.

There were still plenty of parking spaces in the lot at Mount Wilson Elementary School. Since Sunny's busy times were afternoons, she'd requested an early-morning appointment with Mrs. Tuttle. She hadn't wanted to bring Dean along, but over the past few days, he'd insinuated himself so thoroughly into her family life, she'd almost forgotten why she'd objected. Almost.

She sent the twins off to entertain themselves on the playground and entered the classroom.

"Good morning, Ms. McCloud." Her voice booming, Mrs. Tuttle could cower a child at the back of a gymnasium filled with screaming kids. She strode across the room as if she were a drill sergeant and extended her hand. "It's nice to meet the twins' father, Mr. McCloud. Amazing how close a family resem—"

"This is Dean Weylin, Mrs. Tuttle," Sunny quickly interjected. *Now* she remembered a very good reason why she ought to keep Dean and the twins as far apart as possible. At least out of sight of perceptive schoolteachers. "Dr. Weylin is a friend of the family."

"Really?" The teacher looked nonplussed, her studied examination of Dean far too acute for Sunny's liking. "I'm sorry. I simply assumed—"

"A natural mistake, Mrs. Tuttle," Dean said, smoothing things over. It did give him an odd feeling, however, to be categorized as a parent. That term carried a lot of emotional baggage for him. Some good, some bad. "Sunny asked me to come along because we both believe Danny may be having trouble with—"

"Now, if you're going to tell me all about ADD, this Attention Deficient business, and how your twins need to be on medication, I'm going to tell you not to waste your money. It's no more than a fad. I've been teaching third-graders for nearly forty years. Little boys never have been able to sit still more than twenty seconds, and never will. They grow out of it. Eventually."

Dean tensed. "I suspect Danny's problem is more than simply an inability to sit still." He knew the frustration of nerve endings that refused to behave themselves. It'd make anybody jumpy. Dean was having plenty of trouble in the classroom himself. Bulletin board messages were a scramble of letters that made little sense, a painful reminder of his own reading difficulties. He couldn't even cope with third-grade work.

"Mrs. Tuttle, we think Danny may have dyslexia," Sunny said.

"I haven't noticed anything unusual." Multiple layers of wrinkles on Mrs. Tuttle's face shifted downward, as though she'd had too many plastic surgeries and the skin could no longer maintain its resilience. "Danny sometimes reverses letters, of course, and stumbles over words when he reads, but that's not unusual in third grade. By spring—"

"Danny can't read," Dean insisted. "He's having a real problem."

"That's nonsense. Let me get the grade book. Danny's not my most outstanding student, but not the worst, either. You young yuppie parents have to accept that not every child can be a genius. He has a lovely personality and is well liked by the other children. Although he can be a bit disruptive in class from time to time, basically he's doing just fine."

Dean didn't think so.

Mrs. Tuttle seated them around a pint-size table. The chairs were so low, Dean's knees nearly folded up to his chest.

"There, you see," Mrs. Tuttle said. She pointed to a column in her record book of what appeared to be test scores. "Danny's doing as well as many of the other children and Howie's record is even better. I really do think the worst thing parents can do is expect more of their child than their abilities warrant. It's so hard on their fragile egos. We need to encourage our youngsters—"

Speaking very firmly, Sunny said, "I'd like Danny tested for dyslexia."

The teacher blinked and frowned, as if Sunny were a recalcitrant child who hadn't been listening.

Dean knew how much that demand had cost Sunny. As all parents, she had dreams for her sons. In her eyes they were perfect. Admitting there might be a problem had to hurt.

"Well!" Mrs. Tuttle slapped her record book closed. Her cheeks took on a reddish hue, signifying either anger or rising blood pressure. "I do think you ought to listen to someone with experience in these matters. I can't recommend testing for Daniel. Not in this day and age when money is so short and teachers don't even make a decent wage."

"We'll talk to the principal," Dean stated flatly.

"You do that, young man. But it's *my* recommendation he'll listen to. If you want Daniel tested, you'll have to do it privately. I won't stand by and have hundreds of dollars of taxpayers' money wasted." The morning bell rang and she stood. "If you will excuse me."

With all the grace of a herd of miniature rhinoceroses, the children came thundering into the classroom. Danny and Howie made a beeline for their mother.

"Am I in trouble?" Danny asked, his bright blue eyes clouded with worry.

"Of course not, honey." She hugged his already sweaty head against her midsection and palmed

Howie's flushed cheek. "You boys be good today and I'll see you when you get home."

She and Dean left the chaos of the classroom as Mrs. Tuttle tried, somewhat futilely, to bring the youngsters to order.

Sunny fumed. Didn't that woman understand her son's future was worth far more than a few hundred dollars? Admittedly Sunny didn't need another expense to add on top of the cost of the new roof for the roadhouse and Pop's medical bills. But Danny's future was too important to ignore. And if the school wouldn't take care of its responsibility to its students, she would.

With his hand placed at the small of her back, Dean guided her toward the principal's office. The heat of his touch seeped through the fabric of her dress and seared her with his casual possessiveness.

A half hour later, they were back in the school yard and Sunny's temper was about to burst.

"That principal was worse than Mrs. Tuttle! Talk about a namby-pamby bureaucrat. Why should it take *months* to get approval to test Danny? If we wait that long, he could suffer irreparable—"

"Easy, Sunny, we'll get things taken care of," Dean soothed.

"But how?"

"Look, my brother Rick is peripherally involved in the education business. Chances are, a good psychologist specializing in learning disabled kids owes him a favor. I think we ought to check with Rick to see if we can get Danny some *pro bono* diagnostic help. And get it soon."

"I don't want to impose, and I don't need charity." She lifted her chin. She wanted to keep her distance from Dean and his family, not be in their debt. But *hundreds of dollars?* What piggy bank was she going to rob to find that kind of money? And Danny truly couldn't wait, not if he had a serious learning problem.

"There's no harm in asking. Rick's office isn't too far from here. It'd be worth it if you could save a few bucks, and it sure would be a lot faster than waiting for the school district to get its act together."

She eyed him suspiciously. Dean had already offered to pay her medical bills when she'd been hit by that ricocheting bullet. She didn't want him thinking of her and her sons as a charity case. "I don't want you paying for the testing, then telling me the psychologist contributed his time," she warned. "Danny's my problem, not yours. I'll manage somehow."

"Sure you will." His easy shrug came off like a lie.

WEYLIN ENTERPRISES occupied far more than a simple office. Located in an upscale industrial area, the white stucco building boasted a plush reception area filled to overflowing with video game machines.

"What kind of educational work does your brother do?" Sunny asked, incredulous. This looked more like an arcade than any classroom she'd ever seen.

"He's a computer whiz. He calls himself a hacker but he's much more than that. When he was halfway through college, he got bored, so he dropped out. He started developing computer games, sold a few and his business took off. Sometimes I think he'd still rather being playing games than managing a company with two dozen or so employees.''

''Impressive.''

After checking on Richard Weylin's whereabouts, the adolescent receptionist with huge glasses and an endearing smile told them he was in the shop, testing some new hardware. Sunny didn't expect to find the CEO of even a small business sitting beside a young child in a wheelchair, the two of them intently staring at a computer screen on which little green men were shooting rockets at each other and their respective spaceships.

''Keep your eye on the target,'' Rick ordered. ''Then blink.'' In a puff, a spaceship vanished from the screen. ''Atta girl! You got me. But watch out, I'm coming up behind you. I'm gonna shoot. *Blooey!* You weren't quick enough.''

The child giggled and her head lolled to the side. Spacecraft and green men shot off the screen in all directions.

''Hey, no laughing, Marsha. Now my whole army has to regroup!'' Grinning, Rick spotted Dean, and set aside his computer joystick. He told the girl, ''You keep practicing, honey. My big brother is here to check up on me and I have to talk to him. I'll be back in a few minutes to take you on again.''

Dean extended his hand to his brother, affection obvious between the two men who shared a strong family resemblance. Except Rick's hair was long and unkempt, not a mass of tight, unruly curls like Dean's.

"Rick, I want you to meet a friend of mine, Sunny McCloud. She and her grandfather run the roadhouse up on Angeles Crest Highway."

Rick's welcoming smile was a replica of Dean's. He eyed Sunny appreciatively. "I do believe that shot to the head may have finally improved your taste in women, big brother."

A heated flush crept up Sunny's neck. "Nice to meet you, Rick."

Dean gestured to the girl in the wheelchair. "What's going on?"

"Oh, we're working with a bunch of kids who have severely limited mobility. Marsha has very little control of her hand muscles, so a joystick or a keyboard for computer work is out of the question. We're trying to develop a system where she can type by controlling her eye movements and where she focuses. If we can make it work, she'll be able communicate via the computer. Hell, she'll be able to write the great American novel, if she wants to." He glanced over at the girl, his enthusiasm and pride obvious in his expression. "She's as sharp as a tack. We wouldn't want to waste a mind like that."

"What happened to that project for blind people you were working on?" Dean asked.

"We got that one nailed. The first prototype went out the door a month ago with a braille strip that reads whatever is on the screen. It's working without a glitch." He turned to Sunny. "Are you interested in computers?"

She laughed. "I don't think so. I can hardly handle a cash register."

"Hey, computers are easy." He took her by the arm. "Come on, let me show you some of the user-friendly stuff we've got."

"Ease up, Rick," Dean warned. "We came to ask for a referral to an educational specialist for one of Sunny's sons. We want him tested for dyslexia."

"Oh, yeah?" His eyes widened on an unspoken question. "Come on into the office. I'll give you the name and phone number of the guy I've been working with. He's top-notch."

"Sunny's hoping he'll work *pro bono.*"

"I can pay something," she insisted. "It's just that right now—"

"No problem, Sunny. Ralph Alatorre is a good guy. I'll talk to him."

She hated having to ask a favor of anyone, particularly with Dean involved, but her pride would have to take a back seat to her checkbook for the moment. If the snows didn't come early this year, along with the income that came with a super skiing season, more than just her checking account would be in jeopardy. Ownership of the roadhouse could be at stake.

Once in Rick's cluttered office, Dean explained how he had identified that Danny might have a reading problem, and his teacher's reaction to the possibility. Rick was happy to make contact with Dr. Alatorre, who agreed to see Danny the following week at no cost.

Grateful for the psychologist's generosity and Rick's help, Sunny headed for the ladies' room before she and Dean made the return trip up the hill.

Leaning against the doorjamb, arms folded, Dean watched Sunny walk away. She had a nice swing to her hips, he mused, and her legs ranked right up there around a ten. He liked the way her full skirt swayed from side to side, the hem teasing at her nicely shaped calves. Overall, he'd give her a—

"I wasn't kidding when I said your taste had improved," Rick said. "I definitely approve, big bro. When are you going to give her the honor of meeting the folks?"

Dean snapped his attention back to his grinning brother. "Knock it off, Rick. I'm not in any position to introduce a woman to Mother and Dad."

"Is she married?"

"Nope."

"Then what's the matter? Did that gunshot blow away your famous Weylin charm?"

"Oh, I've still got *all* the charm in this family," he conceded pointedly. "I just don't think Sunny or any other woman would want to get hooked up with a functional illiterate."

"Don't be so hard on yourself. You sound like Dad. The doctors said your memory will come back and your dyslexia will probably vanish at the same time."

"Yeah. That's what they said. Problem is, they can't guarantee squat. No one knows how the brain really works or how much damage that bullet actually did inside my head.''

''Well, if Sunny is any example of the changes that have been made, maybe you ought to hope you never fully recover.''

Laughing, Dean punched his brother's shoulder. ''Thanks a lot. Always nice to know I have you on my side.''

THE MIDMORNING TRAFFIC was light going back up the hill. At the roadhouse, Sunny parked her car next to the Forest Service truck Quinn normally drove. Looking grim, he strode out of the café toward them.

Sunny got an uncomfortable feeling in the pit of her stomach. Something was wrong. Quinn never dropped by during the middle of the day unless there was trouble.

''I thought you ought to know,'' he began without preamble. ''There's been another shooting.''

Chapter Six

"Where? When?" Sunny gasped.

"About midmorning." Concern tightened the lines around Quinn's lips. "Someone took a few potshots at a couple of hikers near Switzer Falls."

"Oh, my..." Her hand flew to her mouth. In a steadying, *possessive* gesture, Dean slipped his arm around her waist. To her unending irritation, she was glad he had. "Was anyone hurt?" she asked.

"Fortunately not," Quinn said. "We don't know if we're dealing with a guy who's a lousy shot or some nut who just likes to scare people."

"Neither sounds like a good situation to me," Dean said grimly. "If he's not trying to hit anyone, then he made a mistake when he clipped Sunny's arm."

"Yeah, you're right," Quinn agreed. "But the good news is whoever's running around with a rifle wasn't targeting you two in particular up at the fire lookout. Instead it looks like we're dealing with random acts of violence."

"That's not particularly reassuring." Sunny's stomach roiled on the thought that someone with a rifle could have them in their sights at that very moment and be so hidden by the trees as to be invisible. Even if it was just a prankster with poor eyesight, the possibility made her shudder.

"What are the authorities doing to locate the sniper?" Dean asked.

"We're conducting a search. You'll be hearing a lot of helicopters, I imagine. Unfortunately if the guy doesn't want to be spotted, the forest is a good place to hide. Until we get a good lead and can use some tracking dogs, I don't think we have much chance of catching him." Quinn tunneled his fingers through his hair. "There's another hitch, too."

"What's that?"

"A mountain lion was spotted near the campground earlier this morning."

"Where I'm camped?" Dean asked.

"That's right. We figure she's looking for food or water. Or both. It's been a dry summer."

"Swell," Sunny groaned. "A sniper is on the loose and so is a mountain lion. What do we do now?"

"I'm planning to keep Mindy and Billy pretty close to home until we get a lead on this guy. Or at least until we figure out what he's up to. I thought you might want to do the same with the twins."

"I will. I promise." She shot Dean a troubled look. The prospect of him remaining in the campground, under the circumstances, was a little frightening. Perhaps he'd get the message, pack up and leave. For his own safety, she hoped he would.

Strangely, however, the mere possibility of his departure caused a lonely ache to tighten her chest. She didn't dare examine her emotional reaction too closely. There were some truths she didn't want to face.

IF THE HIKERS hadn't been TV newspeople, the shooting would never have been blown up so big on the five o'clock news. Nor would anyone have heard about the prowling mountain lion. Sunny was sure of it. But, as she well knew, life was not always a rational experience.

Only a few bikers, those who hadn't heard the hyped-up news stories, came to the roadhouse for dinner. The next day and night, no one came at all.

Sunny could almost see her cash flowing in a pathetic green river down the highway. A week or two of this and she would be flat broke.

If only winter would start, maybe that would drive the nut with the rifle into someplace warm and out of her life, and send the lion back where it belonged. But the heat of a late fall lingered on the dust-choked mountainside.

In an effort to relieve some of her frustration—a great deal of which had been brought on by Dean's persistent attention—Sunny decided the next morning to light into her least favorite job. Cleaning the huge commercial oven. Surely that would give her something to think about besides snipers, mountain lions, lack of income and her prolonged celibacy—subjects that had been much on her mind of late.

Midmorning, Dean strolled into the kitchen in search of a decent cup of coffee. He stopped in his tracks. His lips quirked. He'd seen a lot of sexy women in his life, but none in quite such an intriguing and vulnerable position. On her knees, Sunny had climbed halfway inside the oven. Her neat little butt stuck up in the air, a fascinating target that conjured all sorts of interesting images, ones he doubted she would appreciate. She was wearing shorts, and her blouse and waistband had separated, revealing a strip of creamy white skin.

"Now that is definitely a sight worth waking up for," he drawled.

Sunny snapped her head up, bashing the back of her skull against the top of the oven. "Ouch! Oh, shoot!" She pulled her head out of the oven and glared at him. Strands of wayward blond hair framed her flushed face. "Don't you ever knock?"

"Don't need to. You've made me feel right at home here."

"This is not your home, Dr. Weylin. And I'd appreciate a little—"

"There wasn't any coffee in the pot out front." He held up his mug and gave her his most convincing innocent look. "I didn't want to put you to any trouble."

"Oh." Some of the steam went out of her anger. "I didn't see much point in making a pot. We haven't had enough customers in the past couple of days to drink it up." She nodded toward the stove. "There's some left over from breakfast, if you'd like."

"Thanks." He poured the coffee into his mug. The steaming liquid looked dark, thick and bitter, just like the kind he'd learned to drink when he was doing all-nighters as an intern. The thought stopped him. That particular recollection was new to his damaged memory bank. He strained to stretch it into more sights and sounds, pictures of what he'd been doing, the knowledge he'd been gaining. But nothing more came to him.

He shook his head, as if that would dislodge a new memory.

"I didn't say the coffee was fresh," Sunny said defensively.

"Looks great. I've always liked brass monkeys with hair on their chest." He leaned against the stainless-steel counter. "Don't let me keep you from your work."

"It'll wait."

"Strange, after all this time, I still make you nervous."

"You don't make me nervous, and it hasn't been all that long."

"I don't suppose the problem is that you're attracted to me."

"No."

"No, that's not the problem? Or, no, you're not attracted."

"Neither. Both." Her cheeks grew even more flushed. "Could you take your coffee out to the dining room? I need to get on with..."

He hunkered down next to her. The oven cleaner she'd been using had a powerful lemon scent. Her impact on him was several times greater and far more pleasant. "You're trying to make this complicated."

"I'm trying to clean my oven."

"You're a woman, a very attractive woman. I'm a man."

"Congratulations. You just passed Biology 101. Now could I get back to work?"

"You know, there are times when I think I ought to know you."

"You do know me." Her voice trembled slightly. "You've been practically camped in my kitchen for more than a week. Maybe it's time you pulled up stakes."

He frowned, curious about Sunny's reaction to his comment. The synapses in his head that had been awakened by pouring the cup of coffee were stirring around again, but connections continued to elude him. "I think I like the view from this particular campground." He certainly liked the view of her well-shaped thighs and the way she sat with her legs tucked beneath her. The picture of femininity had him wondering which of those skimpy scraps of silk underwear she was wearing today. Bright red would be his choice. "But I wouldn't be adverse to getting a different perspective. How 'bout I take you out to dinner?

We could pick someplace nice. A little wine, soft music . . ."

"I'm the one who cooks dinner, remember? It's how I make my living."

"Given the drop-off in traffic lately, I imagine Pop can manage whatever dinnertime rush you might get."

"No. Thanks." She turned and stuck her head back into the oven, leaving Dean staring at a very appealing part of anatomy belonging to a very determined woman.

A woman who was doing her damnedest to keep her distance from him.

He remembered enough about his past and his relationships with women to know few had turned down a dinner invitation. He was baffled as to why Sunny would be the rare exception.

But he'd been effectively told to get lost. At the moment it seemed the wisest thing to do. Maybe consuming high doses of caffeine would jog his memory banks.

Sunny breathed a heavy sigh of relief when Dean finally left the kitchen, then choked on the pungent oven cleaning fumes. She was crazy to allow him anywhere near the roadhouse. Or her children. With frantic awareness, she sensed he was beginning to remember bits and pieces of his past. Their history—which she didn't want restored to his memory.

It was like living with a ticking time bomb. Once he was able to put all the pieces together, there'd be an explosion. She and her sons would be at the center of the blast. People could get hurt, lives damaged beyond repair. Lord, what a mess she'd gotten herself into.

Taking her sponge, she swiped angrily at the grease on the oven wall. To even consider going out to a romantic dinner with Dean was pure lunacy. Candles. Champagne. Soft music. Except she could remember one other time, the first time....

She had been so giddy in love that night she'd actually flirted with the valet who had helped her out of Dean's Corvette.

"Hey, watch that stuff," Dean warned as he slipped his arm possessively around her waist.

"A girl can still look, can't she, even when she's with the handsomest med student in town?"

"Okay, you can look, but don't touch." He pulled open the heavy door to the restaurant. A teasing smile canted his lips.

Laughing, she swept past him. "I won't, I promise." That was an easy vow to keep. Her love for Dean filled her heart so full, there wasn't a speck of room for any other man.

They were seated in a secluded booth draped by red velvet that matched the upholstered seats. The single candle on the table was more for effect than light, and there was a hushed sense of elegance as both the well-dressed diners and waiters in tuxedos spoke in quiet, intimate voices.

"Do you think I ought to ask Pop to remodel the roadhouse in this decor?" she asked, stifling a nervous giggle. She'd never eaten in a restaurant quite this fancy.

"I'm not so sure the bikers would appreciate candles and tablecloths." His hand covered hers on the tabletop in a warm caress that matched the heated look in his eyes.

"You're probably right." Dean certainly looked at home, though. He was wearing a dark suit that fit his broad shoulders as though it was hand tailored; his tie was made of expensive silk. The maître d' had been particularly cordial, calling him by name and inquiring about his parents. Sunny hadn't met his family yet, but sensed Dean came from wealth. Not that she cared one way or the other. She admired him for the goals he had set and his ambition. Too often the young men she dated had neither.

A waiter arrived and Dean smoothly ordered a champagne that sounded expensive and tickled her nose when she drank from the fluted glass.

"Do you always bring your girlfriends here to impress them?" she asked.

"Is it working?"

She shrugged. *"Should I not admit Denny's is about the fanciest restaurant I've ever been to?"*

"I'll let you in on a little secret. I brought you here because you're not jaded. You're honest and open and say exactly what you think. Unlike some other women I've known. And I was hoping to impress you."

"Then I'll tell you this is lovely, but I'd be just as happy to be eating dinner with you at Joe's Greasy Spoon, or having take-out Chinese." She squeezed his hand. *"It's you I want to be with. Where doesn't matter."*

Sunny ate her meal leisurely, savoring the flavors of wine and roasted lamb, relishing the feeling of anticipation that was more heady than any alcoholic beverage.

After they'd finished the last of a sinfully rich chocolate cheesecake, Dean asked, "Would you like to see my apartment? My roommates are away during the summer break. We'd have the place to ourselves."

Sunny knew he was suggesting more than a tour of his condo near the medical school. With any other man, she would have declined the invitation. But Dean was different. Almost from the first moment she'd met him, when he'd come up to the roadhouse from the campground in search of a meal he hadn't cooked himself, she'd known that he was the man who would steal her heart.

That night, she willingly gave it to him.

"HEY, HON, have the fumes gotten to you?"

Sunny snapped out of her reverie to find Mindy Petersen standing over her. Her body still pulsed with the heavy sense of anticipation she'd felt so many years ago. The same aching need. The oven was as clean as if it had just come from the factory. She'd been so totally absorbed in her thoughts, memories that still throbbed through the here and now, she hadn't heard her friend come into the kitchen.

"Hi, Mindy." Picking up her sponge, Sunny levered herself a little unsteadily to her feet. She blinked away the images that had been so real to her only moments ago. "I thought Quinn was keeping you close to home until the sniper is caught."

"Oh, I took Billy to school this morning because I had a doctor's appointment. Since I was out anyway, I thought I'd stop by to see how you all were doing."

"Business is impossibly slow, but we're okay. At least, nobody's shot at us lately."

With easy familiarity, Mindy poured out the dregs of the morning coffee and made a new pot. "Dean Weylin is in the dining room. He said he was studying, but I think he's guarding the place."

"I know. He's practically moved in."

"Hmm. Nice roommate." She grinned.

"Pop hired him to help around the place. It hardly seems necessary when we don't have any customers."

"I wouldn't mind having a man like Dean hanging around my house. Of course, Quinn might object. He's a bit possessive."

Sunny laughed. She rinsed the sponge in the sink beneath the window that looked out over the backyard and up the hill. She wished the water could dash a cooling chill over her heated memories. "I'd be happy to loan him to you."

"You sound like you're awfully eager to get rid of the man."

"I am."

"Is that because he's the twins' father?"

The sponge slipped from her hand; a roaring sound filled her head and all the blood drained from her face. Without turning around, Sunny stuttered, "Wh-what do you mean?"

"I'm not blind, hon. The first time I saw him I thought he looked familiar. The more I thought about it . . . well, your twins look so much like that man it's spooky. Particularly their eyes. I've never seen such clear blue eyes on anyone—"

"Please, Mindy." She whirled. "This is not something I want to discuss."

"I didn't mean to pry. It's just that . . ." She frowned. "The boys don't know?"

"No." She shook her head. "Dean doesn't know, either."

Mindy sank slowly onto the chair at the table. "How is that possible? Is he blind?"

"Maybe men don't notice things like eye color." Or hair so filled with cowlicks it mimicked his own.

"But he's got to remember you, hon. It wouldn't take a genius to put two and two together. I think even Quinn's noticed, he just hasn't said anything yet."

"Oh, God, Mindy, you can't let him say anything to Dean. Not till I—"

"What isn't Quinn supposed to tell me?"

Sunny's heart slammed against her rib cage. Dean was standing in the kitchen doorway, his expression open, interested and dangerously curious. She opened her mouth to speak, but no sound came out. What could she say? It was too soon for him to discover her secret.

Mindy's gaze darted from Dean to Sunny and back again. "Ah, Quinn's been thinking you might want to move your camping van up here, next to the roadhouse. For Sunny and the twins' protection."

"No." Sunny choked on the word.

He eyed them as though he suspected that hadn't been the original topic. "Not a bad idea. I could park around back, out of the way."

"I'm sure you'd be more comfortable staying at the campground," Sunny protested.

"Actually, after all the flap about the sniper and wandering mountain lions, the campground is deserted. I might be the one who'd be safer if I camped out back."

Sunny's conscience pricked her. She'd known that and tried not to think about it. The possibility that the sniper would come after Dean sent a shiver of dread through her. And the image of the lion attacking... She swallowed hard.

"Well then, that's all settled." Mindy smiled brightly. "I gotta run, guys. I'll see you both later."

"No, wait!" Sunny cried, but it was too late. Mindy was gone, a new conspirator determined to get her and Dean together. An impossible situation.

"I'll bring up my van this evening," Dean said.

"I'd rather you didn't."

"I know. That's probably why it's exactly what I'm going to do. You bring out the worst in me, Sunny McCloud." His gaze roved over her with blatant sexual innuendo. "Or maybe it's the best."

DEAN LEANED HIS ELBOW on the bar and sipped his beer while Pop conducted an inventory of the roadhouse's liquor supply.

"I could use your help, Pop."

"How's that?" The old man was crouched behind the bar counting bottles.

"I get the feeling Sunny doesn't have as much fun as she deserves."

"Might be."

"I'd like to change that."

Pop peered up at him from his crouched position. "Used to be she smiled a whole lot and laughed, too. Then along came this guy who broke her heart. Wouldn't want that to happen again."

"Neither would I, Pop. And I'd never do anything to hurt her. Not intentionally. I'd just like to see her smile more often."

Pop gave him a strange look. For an instant, Dean felt a twinge of guilt, as if he'd been the one to take Sunny's smile away. He shrugged off the thought because it didn't make any sense.

Scratching at the fringe of hair at the back of his head, Pop said, "Reckon she dotes on them twins more than anything else these days. Figure if you was to offer them youngsters a trip to an amusement park, she'd find it all-fired hard to refuse."

"You think she'd go along?"

"As I recall, there's nothing that didn't used to make her smile more than a rolly coaster."

"Yeah, but would she go with me?"

"I think she wouldn't leave them boys alone with you any more than a mother hen would leave her chicks in the clutches of a big, bad wolf."

Dean wasn't sure he liked being compared to the villain of Little Red Riding Hood. But still, it was a start. Maybe if he could get her away from the road-house—and out of range of the sniper—she'd relax a little. Then they'd have a chance to get acquainted.

That idea he liked a whole lot.

"THAT'S IT!" Pop announced, directing Dean as he backed his van into position behind the roadhouse. "Pull her back another foot or so. Keep comin'. You got it!" He waved his arms to halt the vehicle.

The van lurched to a stop. The brake lights flared, Dean shifted into park and cut the motor.

Sunny gritted her teeth.

She hated having Dean camped twenty feet from her house, practically within spitting distance. How on earth was she going to avoid him now? His nearness would plague her every minute, day *and* night.

"Well, missy, what do you think?" Pop puffed out his chest as if he'd done something marvelous and smiled smugly at her.

"I think you're being just a little too helpful when it comes to Dean Weylin."

"Now then, don't go gettin' all cactus prickery on me. I just happen to believe in them family values everybody's talkin' about these days. Cain't fault me for that, ken you?"

"Dean is *not* part of this family," she hissed.

"Reckon that might change, you give him a chance."

She'd given him a chance once. He hadn't been interested, and it had nearly broken her heart. She couldn't set herself up for heartbreak again. Nor could she subject her boys to the same devastating sense of rejection.

"Pop, you've got to quit meddling in my life. And Dean's. He's working very hard to regain his skills so he can be a doctor again. That's what he wants. Not me." She and the boys meant no more than a pleasant interlude to him. A diversion. That's all she'd ever been. She'd seen little indication that the future would be different.

And in her heart she was afraid to even hope.

Dean hopped out of the van and waved the boys over from the safety of the back porch. "You fellows tell your mom where we're gonna go this weekend? *If* it's okay with her, of course."

The twins looked up at her, their eyes alight with enthusiasm.

"Dean says he'll take us to Magic Mountain," Danny announced. "And you can come, too."

"We can ride all the roller coasters and stuff," Howie added, his glasses slightly askew. He readjusted them with the push of a finger. "All the big stuff."

Stunned, Sunny whipped an accusing look toward Dean. "Was it your idea?"

"They picked the amusement park."

"You should have asked me before—"

"I figured you'd say no if I asked, so I talked to Pop instead."

"Pop is not their mother," she hissed. "I make the decisions—"

"Ah, Mom, we'll have fun," Danny whined. "You know how much you like to go on scary rides. Dean says he does, too."

"But the last time—" She clamped her mouth shut before she gave away too much. Dean suffered from motion sickness. The one time he'd taken her to the Magic Mountain, at her request, he'd become quite ill. Though the day itself had turned out to be one of the most wonderful she could remember—after he'd recovered from the roller-coaster ride.

Her eyes narrowed. Unless Dean's head injury had corrected his old problem with motion sickness, he'd just left himself wide open for the best kind of revenge. She'd teach him a thing or two about undercutting a mother's authority.

Besides, she thought a little wickedly, she hadn't ridden on Colossus in years. And she certainly wouldn't want to deny her sons the rare opportunity to visit an amusement park.

THINGS WEREN'T WORKING out as Dean had planned.

Colossus whipped them around a curve, then dropped them through space. Dean's stomach threatened rebellion. He felt disoriented, his inner ear unable to keep up with the speed and quick changes in direction.

Meanwhile, Danny was sitting beside him, delighted with the unsettling motion, the constant rocking, the pressure of increased G-forces. In the seat behind them, Sunny was having the time of her life.

He could hear her joyful screams, her laughter as she and Howie enjoyed the fun together.

Grimacing, Dean wondered how he was supposed to get Sunny into a romantic mood when any minute he was probably going to seriously embarrass himself.

The sled came to a stop. He staggered as he got out and swallowed hard.

"That was neat, wasn't it, Dean?" Danny raved.

"Terrific. Where's your mom?"

"She's coming."

Dean stood rooted in place. Waiting. And weaving.

"Dean, are you all right?" Sunny's soft voice slowed some of the spinning inside Dean's head. But not the waves of nausea that rose in his throat.

"Yeah. Sure. Great ride, uh?" He forced a smile.

"You look like you're about to pass out."

"No. I'm fine. Really."

Sunny didn't think so. Dean was as pale as a ghost, and there was a sheen of sweat on his face. The sweet taste of revenge suddenly tasted a little bitter. And this was only their first ride of the day.

She slid her arm through his. "Come on, boys. Dean needs to get his bearings for a minute."

"Just give me a minute..." He walked unsteadily toward the exit.

She found them an empty bench in the shade and made Dean sit down.

"Can we go again, Mom?" Howie asked eagerly. "Can we?"

"Not right now, honey. We're going to rest here for a few minutes."

"Aw, gee, Mom. The line is—"

"Howie! I told you no. Now sit—"

Dean shook off her concern. "You guys go ahead. I'll catch up with you later."

"I'm not going to leave you, Dean. Just relax a minute." She dug into her fanny pack and found some money. "Boys, there's a man selling lemonade right over there. Can you see him?"

Easily diverted by the promise of a treat, both boys nodded.

"I want you to buy us each something cold to drink and then come right back here. Can you do that?"

"Yeah, sure, Mom." Danny took the money and turned to leave.

"Pay attention to where you're going so you won't get lost. And walk, don't run," she called after them, but it was already too late as they dashed past slower pedestrians.

She sighed.

"You shouldn't have let them go off on their own."

"They'll be fine. I can see them from here." She sat down beside Dean. Feeling guilty and unable to resist offering some comfort, she smoothed his hair back from his forehead, much as she would have for one of her sons. "Is your head giving you trouble?"

"More like my stomach. I don't know what's wrong. I've been on that ride before. I know I have." His forehead pleated. "With a girl," he said thoughtfully. "I remember . . ."

Sunny's heart skipped a beat and a panic attack threatened as she could almost see him putting one more piece of the past together. At least on one occasion—probably the only one—she'd been the girl he'd ridden with on Colossus. "Don't think about it now." *Don't ruin a perfect day by remembering.*

"This kind of a ride shouldn't make me sick."

Instinctively, she checked on the twins, who were standing in line.

"It can happen to anyone. Maybe it was something you ate." Normally Dean was a quietly macho man, rarely showing any weakness, fearless in everything he did—except riding on roller coasters. It tugged at Sunny's nurturing instincts to see him hurting now and know she was responsible. She suspected that was a dangerous feeling to have, perhaps even her penance for not wanting his memory to return.

While she kept an eye on the boys, Dean caught her hand, taking it gently, and slowly examining her fingers, then turning it to study her palm. The contrast between his long, tapered fingers—those of a skilled surgeon—and her more feminine hand was striking.

As he raised her hand to his lips, her breathing grew shallow. She felt the moist pressure of his mouth on the sensitive surface of her palm and had to stifle a groan.

"Dean, please—"

His eyes darkened to a deep blue. "Strange. Sometimes I get this incredible sense of déjà vu and I don't know why."

Like an invisible strand of memory, the tension pulled taut between them. The secret of the past vibrated around Sunny's heart, threatening to reveal itself in a word, a kiss. God help her, she was falling in love with Dean Weylin all over again.

Then fear crowded in around her, dampening the impulse to tell him the truth. Too soon! she mentally cried. She'd been a fool once. This time she had her boys to think about. She didn't dare risk their heartbreak, too.

Painfully she tore her gaze away from Dean and slipped her hand from his grasp. The sight of her twins running toward her, lemonade sloshing from the paper cups, blurred through her tears.

Chapter Seven

Holding the pencil tight, Danny bent over the paper. He scrunched up his mouth and tried hard to copy the drawing just exactly like the one the doctor had given him. He hated being here, in this funny office with desks and books and the smell of old magazines. He wished his mom and Dean hadn't brought him. Now everybody was gonna know he was dumb.

He'd copied the picture wrong. He knew he had. He couldn't get those squiggly lines to look right. He never could. They kept jumping around like they were worms.

He used the pencil eraser to erase what he'd done, making a jagged hole in the paper. The doctor didn't say anything. He just sat there looking smart, as if reading and stuff like that should be easy for anyone. Unless they didn't have a brain in their heads.

If the kids at school found out he was stupid, they'd all make fun of him. It was bad enough that they laughed when he messed up on the blackboard and ol'

Mrs. Tuttle yelled at him. But she yelled at every-body.

This would be worse.

Biting his lower lip, he tried again. Howie wasn't stupid. His brother could do almost anything, except maybe fixing a bird whose wing was broken or finding gold. But he never told anybody Danny was dumb. It was their secret, one they never talked about much. But now everybody would know.

A tear plopped onto the paper. He scrubbed at it with his fist to make the wet spot go away, then swiped at his eyes with back of his hand. Only sissies cried.

If his mom found out how stupid he was, maybe even she wouldn't love him anymore.

SUNNY SAT DOWN on one of the upholstered chairs in the waiting room of the psychologist's office so she'd be eye level with her troubled son.

"The doctor's the one who's dumb," Danny insisted. He stood in the middle of the room, right where he'd come to an angry halt after their talk with the doctor had revealed the discouraging results of the testing. Planting his fists on his hips, Danny jutted his jaw out at a stubborn angle. "I was tricking him, see? He's so stupid, he didn't even get the joke."

Her heart breaking, Sunny tugged Danny to her and lifted him, against his will, to hold him on her lap. She hugged him tight. "Honey, nobody is calling anyone stupid. You're having a problem learning to read. That doesn't make you dumb or stupid. It just means you need extra help."

"I don't want any extra help. I *hate* school! It stinks."

"Hey, tiger, it's going to be all right," Dean said, lifting the boy's chin so he'd be forced to look at him.

His father, Sunny thought, desperate to share with the man who had helped to create her son some of the burden that had been laid on her shoulders. Yet she didn't dare admit her need to anyone, and especially not to herself. She'd been a single mother too long, had struggled too hard, to give in now in a moment of weakness.

"You've seen me copying the words out of that big textbook I've got, haven't you?" Dean asked Danny.

"Yeah. So what?" He scowled.

"I'm doing it because I can't read any better than you can. Just like you, I've got a form of dyslexia."

Danny's trembling anger eased, his muscles relaxed and his eyes widened. "You do?"

"You bet. And it's frustrating as hell, isn't it?"

"But you're a doctor. You've got to be able to read—"

"That bullet I took in the head sort of scrambled my brains. The electrical circuits don't work as well as they used to. The same thing probably happened to you at birth. All those connections in your brain didn't quite go together right. It wasn't your fault then, when you were born, any more than it's my fault some gang-banger took a shot at me. And it doesn't mean either of us is stupid."

Danny didn't look convinced. "Howie doesn't have any problem with reading, and we were born together. He's one of the smartest guys in the class."

"Yeah, well, maybe the girls don't like him as well as they like you. Everybody's got some kind of a disability."

The slightest curl lifted Danny's lips. "We don't like girls yet."

"You will, chum. Trust me on that." Dean shot Sunny a look that suggested his recently acquired learning disability hadn't affected his appreciation of women.

Echoing Dean's action, Danny looked up at Sunny. His chin trembled. "Are you mad at me, Mom?"

"Oh, sweetheart, no." Tears burned at the back of her eyes and a wave a guilt swept over her for whatever failing of hers might have contributed to Danny's problem. "You are so special to me, and I love you so much, I could never be mad at you. Not because of this. Not ever."

"You were pretty mad when I knocked over the ladder."

She frowned at him. "I thought that was Howie."

He shrugged as if the admission was inconsequential. "Sometimes I get him to take the blame for stuff when it's my fault. He knows sometimes I'm a geek."

"Daniel Har—" She caught herself and stumbled over the name. "Daniel McCloud! I never want to hear you call yourself that name again. You're a wonderful little boy and you're going to be a wonderful man. Did you know Einstein was dyslexic? And Thomas Edison? And . . . and . . . Cher?"

"Cher?" Danny complained. "Oh, yuck. She's a girl!"

Sunny pulled her son even more tightly into her arms. "Honey, we're going to have the best time learning how to deal with this. Dr. Alatorre gave us a whole bunch of things we can do together, even things where Howie can help. We'll get the school involved. I promise, everything will be all right."

Easing Danny off her lap, Sunny went to the receptionist counter. She pulled her checkbook from her purse.

"How much do I owe the doctor?" she asked.

"Oh, it's all taken care of, Ms. McCloud." The young woman's smile revealed a set of teeth so perfect they belonged in a toothpaste commercial.

Sunny glanced toward Dean for confirmation that the bill had been paid—wanting to know by whom. He was staring at her with the strangest look on his face. Her heart thudded. She'd just made a huge gaffe nearly saying Danny's middle name aloud.

He shrugged absently, then gazed back at Danny. Again she had the feeling she'd done something terribly wrong.

"Rick said he'd arrange the evaluation *pro bono,*" he said.

Thoughtful, she nodded. Given a checkbook with a balance that always hovered on the dangerously low side, Sunny couldn't very well object to whatever arrangements had been made. Just this morning she'd confirmed that her bank account was as dismal as her records showed. But in some less practical part of her brain, she cringed at the thought of being obligated to any member of the Weylin family.

"Okay, if I don't owe anything..." She smiled a weak thank-you to the receptionist, then took Danny's hand.

Dean followed Sunny and her son out of the office. The day was blistering hot, the asphalt driveway softening under the noon sun. He loosened his tie and released the top button of his shirt. It would feel good to get back to the cooler air of the mountains.

A lot had been learned during their visit to the psychologist's office that morning. But what puzzled him the most was the way Sunny had abruptly cut Danny's middle name short, as if it was something she didn't want Dean to hear.

Now why, he wondered, would she want to keep that a secret? And why did she seem so uniquely familiar to him?

THERE WAS A LOT of giggling going on at the homework table in Sunny's kitchen. However distracting it might be, she could hardly complain.

Since Danny had officially been diagnosed as dyslexic three days ago, Dean had taken over supervising his studies every afternoon. He managed to add this new activity between his "waitering" duties for the few faithful customers who were slowly returning to the roadhouse in spite of the persistent stories of snipers and mountain lions. He'd made a game of learning, both for himself and his son. *His son,* she thought. How ironic.

She smiled as Howie drilled them both, using the colorful set of plastic alphabet letters Dean had purchased as part of the tactile training the doctor had recommended. In some magical way, Dean seemed to have a natural instinct for drawing the best from the twins. Giving Howie responsibility fed his ego while not diminishing Danny's needs. Dean's admission of his own shortcomings seemed to be the glue that held the entire project together.

Not many men would be able to do that, she realized. Nine years ago she never would have guessed Dean would have had enough courage to reveal his weaknesses.

"Come on, Danny," Howie encouraged. "Dean did it. Now it's your turn to put those four letters in the right order."

Munching on a potato chip, Danny hesitantly slid the plastic letters into a row.

"Looks right to me," Dean announced.

"Me, too," Howie agreed, slapping his brother a high five.

However much he had changed for the better, Sunny decided Dean's visual perception must have been seriously affected by the gunshot wound. Anyone looking at the three of them together would know they were closely related. The genes ran so true, from their cowlicky hair and eye color, to their quirky smiles, she wondered if she had contributed anything at all to twins' gene pool. Dean had to be practically blind not to see that the boys were his children.

Unless he didn't want to acknowledge them, she thought with a painful knot twisting in her chest.

Pop came into the kitchen through the swinging door.

"That there sure is a purty sight," he said, nodding toward the trio at the table as another burst of masculine laughter filled the room.

"Yes," she conceded.

"Could be that hit on the head changed that young fella in more ways than one."

"Possibly."

"Maybe, right about now, the one what needs to change things is you, missy. It kin be mighty cold on a winter's night when all you've got to curl up with is a stubborn streak."

Even if she agreed with Pop, how could she stroll up to Dean and casually announce that Danny and Howie were his sons? Dean didn't remember her nor their summer together. As far as she could tell, he was still determined to regain his medical skills. That would mean he would leave the mountains—and her—as soon as he was able. In the process he'd be rejecting the twins, too, perhaps scarring them for life. That would be intolerable.

Nine years ago she'd known it would be wrong to hold Dean back. It wasn't clear that the situation had changed all that much.

Worse, an even darker fear lurked at the back of her mind. What if Dean rejected *her* again but claimed his sons, demanding custody? How could she possibly take that risk?

Another burst of laughter came from the table, this one longer and louder than the others.

In spite of herself, Sunny smiled. "Whatever are the three of you up to?"

Dean turned. The boyish sparkle in his eyes was pure, unadulterated mischief. "We're making up gross words for Becky Ragsdale. Danny's going to write her a love letter using them."

"I am not!" Danny protested, laughing as he poked Dean on the arm. "You're going to write mushy ones to Mom!"

"Now that there is a fine idea," Pop chimed in. "Womenfolk always got a soft spot for sweet words."

"Wait a minute," Sunny sputtered. "Why is it I feel like I'm outnumbered?"

"Because you are." Dean's lips canted into a sexy grin, as he tipped his chair back onto two legs and folded his arms across his chest. "Us guys have to stick together. Majority rules."

"Yeah, Mom. Look at all these neat words Dean and Danny made." Howie pushed his brother out of the way so she'd get a better view of the tabletop and the bright plastic letters. "See, here's *boobs* and *butt* and *bottom.*"

"I added the word *cute,* " Dean announced proudly. "I distinctly remember how you looked when—"

Her face flushing with embarrassment, Sunny tossed a hot pad in Dean's direction just to shut him up. "Some role model you make, Weylin! You're supposed to be teaching Danny the vocabulary words in the text, not making up new ones."

"It's called free association."

"It's called picking on me," she countered.

"Only because we love you, Mom."

"He's got that right," Pop agreed.

Sunny rolled her eyes. What an impossible situation, what a wonderful feeling, to be teased by the *four* men who she most loved.

The phone rang. With a shake of her head, she picked up the instrument. "Cloud High Roadhouse, Sunny McCloud speaking."

"Miss McCloud, this is Elmo Durand, principal of Mount Wilson school. As Daniel may have told you, we've been testing him the past few days."

"No, he didn't mention—"

"Mrs. Tuttle and I have consulted, and we've reached a decision as to the best way to proceed. We think Daniel should be put back a year to the second grade. That will give him a chance to catch up."

Sunny's forehead tightened into a worried frown. "What . . . about Howie?" she stammered.

"He's doing fine right where he is, Ms. McCloud. We wouldn't think of disrupting his academic progress."

Sunny knew the principal kept on talking, his voice buzzing in her ear as he made a case for the unilateral decision the school had made. But she couldn't respond with any coherent words. Her head pounded and she had trouble drawing a breath. All she could think about was how devastated Danny would be, and she wondered how she could possibly explain to him that he would be separated from his brother.

"We'd like you to come in on Monday to discuss this matter, but I'm sure you'll be in agreement when you know all the facts," Mr. Durand announced. "The weekend will give Daniel plenty of time to adjust to the idea, and I'm sure the transition will go quite smoothly next week." Then the principal proceeded to expound at length on the experience and skill of Danny's new second-grade teacher.

When she finally hung up, Sunny discovered four pairs of curious eyes staring at her.

Dean reacted first. "What's wrong, Sunny?" Big and strong and tall, he walked across the kitchen toward her. His shoulders were broad enough to carry the weight of her problems, his chest so rock solid she could bury her face in his strength and sob her heart out. But she didn't have the right.

The twins were her responsibility, and hers alone. They had been for more than nine years.

She gazed up into Dean's eyes. Fear and indecision filled her throat. Never in her life had single parenthood rested so heavily on her shoulders, nor had she ever wanted so much to reach out for help. Dean's help.

Her gaze shifted to Danny at the table. It was her job—hers alone—to tell her son the school's decision that had the power to shatter his fragile young ego if she faltered. How could she choose the right words to give him strength? What if she failed?

With legs turned to lead, she walked to the table and knelt in front of Danny. She touched her son's cheek in a loving caress. "Honey, that was Mr. Durand from school. They know you're having some trouble reading…and they think…" The words felt like a lie and were as painfully sharp in her throat as if she'd swallowed razor blades. "They want to help you, and the best way they can do that is to put you back to second grade."

"No-o-o!" Danny screamed. His face turned beet red. "I'm not a baby! I won't go back. I won't!" He slammed away from the table, knocking over a chair in the process, and ran from the room.

Sunny felt sure her heart would break at the pain and horrifying shame she'd seen in her son's eyes.

DEAN KNEW SUNNY had waited until her son had settled down after an uneaten dinner and bedtime before she went outside to escape the emotional tension caused by the school's decision. Only then did he go in search of her. He wasn't sure how he could help. He simply knew he had to try.

Sunny and her boys had become far too important to him to ignore the turmoil they were all experiencing, a situation he had brought to the crisis point by being the first to suspect Danny had a learning disability.

If it hadn't been for his own problems, he might never have noticed that the boy and he shared an unfortunate bond.

The half-moon cast shadows almost as bright as day, as he followed her up a rocky trail behind the roadhouse. The night air was still, with only the occasional sound of a car passing on the road to break the silence, or the swift sound of night wings across the sky. Old pine needles crunched under his footsteps, leaving their dusty scent hanging on the breathless wind.

"Sunny?" he said softly, not wanting to startle her.

When she didn't respond, he came up behind her and slid his arms around her waist. Compliant, she leaned her head against his shoulder. A sigh shuddered through her body.

A memory stirred in the shattered remnants of his brain as he caught the sweet scent of alpine freshness that surrounded her. With almost a physical effort, he pressed for the elusive details. But all he could imagine was the feel of her in the here and now in his arms.

"I'm sorry, Sunny. I feel like this mess with Danny is partly my fault."

She tensed. "Why... Why would you say that?"

"Because I stuck my nose into your business. If I'd left well enough alone, maybe he'd—"

"No. I wish I'd known sooner. Maybe I could have gotten him special tutoring. Done something... Anything."

"Call the principal back tomorrow. Maybe there's still a chance to make some other arrangement."

"I don't know... Mr. Durand caught me so off guard. A mother's supposed to..." Her breath caught on a sob.

Dean turned her in his arms. Framing her face, he wiped his thumbs across her cheeks, catching the trail of tears. The psychologist had been right. Tactile sense was a powerful learning tool. He could feel the contour of Sunny's cheekbones, the texture of her flawless skin, its warmth and resiliency. And he sensed, at a very deep level, her vulnerability.

"You're a terrific mom." The words formed thickly in his throat, both in admiration and with an emotion he was reluctant to name. "You'll get through this. You all will."

"Sometimes it's so hard."

"Let me help." In spite of his best intentions, he lowered his head and found her full lips, kissing her softly.

She moaned and broke away. "I can't . . . we . . . I'm sorry!"

As her son had fled the truth earlier in the day, Sunny ran away, down the hill and into the roadhouse, the screen door slamming shut behind her.

Dean stood looking after her until her shadow was nothing but a memory and the phantoms of his past teased once again at the corners of his mind.

DANNY JUMPED at the sound of the back door slamming. He lay on his stomach, his head resting on his arm, staring across the dark room toward his brother's bed.

"Are you awake, Howie?"

"Mmm. I guess."

"I'm gonna run away tomorrow."

"Why'd you wanna do that? Second grade won't be so bad."

A tear squeezed out of Danny's eye. "Yeah, it will. They're all babies."

There was a long pause before Howie said, "Where're you gonna go?"

"I dunno. Someplace."

"How're you gonna eat and stuff?"

"While Mom was outside, I sneaked downstairs and got a whole bunch of candy bars and chips and stuff from the behind the bar. I put 'em in my backpack instead of my books. I'm not gonna go to school in the morning."

"Mom's gonna be mad."

"Not if I find enough gold so she's rich enough that she won't ever have to work again and Pop won't have to worry about doctor bills. And I won't have to go to school, either. It won't matter if I can't read."

Howie moved restlessly on his bed. "I wouldn't mind finding some gold, too. Want me to come with you?"

Danny smiled. He'd been too scared to admit it, but he'd hoped his brother would go along. He didn't much like the thought of being all alone in the mountains. "Yeah. We'll go half-and-half on all the gold we find."

He rolled over then and was asleep almost as soon as he closed his eyes.

Chapter Eight

The school bus lumbered past the roadhouse, its diesel engine straining up the steep grade, and Sunny glanced at the clock over the stove. Four-fifteen. Right on time. The twins would be roaring in through the back door any minute now, home from school.

Irritation had her on edge. Mr. Durand, the school principal, still hadn't responded to the message she'd left that morning. Hadn't it occurred to him that her son's future was important? His being moved back to second grade the most critical thing that had ever happened in his young life? She wasn't about to let that happened without a lot of discussion.

She fumed at the feeling that both she and the best interests of her son were being ignored. If the principal didn't get back to her before Monday, she'd be on the phone to the superintendent. To the whole damn school board, if necessary. Danny was too important a person, too vulnerable, to be fobbed off by some educational bureaucrat. Kids with disabilities had rights, too.

Dean shoved in through the swinging door to the kitchen. "Hey, where are the boys? I've come up with these really gross vocabulary words they'll love."

"You're awful," Sunny laughed. "But you certainly know how to get the twins' attention. I can just imagine what your mother went through raising you and your brother."

"I doubt she ever noticed. Between charity affairs and the country club, she was never home." He lifted his shoulders in an unconcerned shrug. "It was the cook we gave a hard time to. I remember one time we went down to a butcher shop a few blocks away and bought a couple of pounds of innards. Then we—"

"No! I don't want to know," she sputtered. Her stomach roiled at the creative possibilities little boys could conjure. "Maybe next time I'll be blessed with girls."

"I don't know if that would be such a blessing." Sauntering up to her, Dean rearranged her braid in front of her shoulder. His touch was feather light and temptingly sensual. "With girls you have to watch out for some guy who's going to take advantage of them."

"Yes," she whispered a little breathlessly, her eyes wide, her heart tumbling as she recalled their kiss last night. She wished, in spite of all good reason, that he would kiss her again.

"A combination of kids sounds like the best way to go. A couple of boys. A couple of girls. That would keep the odds even."

Instantly she envisioned two little towhead girls with Dean's bright blue eyes grinning up at her from their cribs. She almost gasped, the image was so intense. So real. And so completely unattainable. "I didn't know you liked big families."

"I'm not even sure I've given it any thought. Until now." His gaze swept over her face, bringing a flush to her cheeks. "Though I confess, it doesn't seem like all that bad an idea."

"I always wanted brothers and sisters."

He raised his hand and his fingertips mapped her face in a slow caress. "I would have been happy to loan you mine. Most of the time, Rick was a pest."

"I like him. He's doing some wonderful work with those disabled children."

"Yeah, well, that doesn't mean he wasn't a nuisance when we were kids."

"But you like him now?"

"Actually I do. He's overcome a lot, including a ton of disparaging words from our parents. He was definitely a slow starter. Sort of like Danny, I suppose."

"Your brother had trouble in school?"

"The folks thought he was lazy. The fact is, I saw him working a lot harder than I ever had to, and still his grades weren't all that good. Except at math. When he got into computers it was like a light had gone on inside his head. Too bad Dad has never appreciated what Rick can do."

The chill of awareness slid down Sunny's spine. The psychologist had questioned her about family history. It had never occurred to her that Danny's dyslexia might have come from the Weylin side of the family. The *brilliant* side. Nor had she dared asked Dean any questions during the interview.

He lowered his head toward hers, temptingly close. He was going to kiss her. And she wanted—

Planting her palms on his unyielding chest, she said, "The boys are going to burst through that door any minute..." She frowned. The bus had gone past several minutes ago. Long enough so the boys— "In fact, they should have been here..." She ducked away from Dean and walked to the screen door. A niggling sense of foreboding nagged at her awareness as she wondered what exotic bug or road-injured creature had distracted her children now. Usually the boys were starved for an afternoon snack and nothing would delay their raid on the refrigerator or the potato-chip display.

"What's wrong?" Dean asked.

"The twins. They should have..." She pushed open the screen door and went outside. There was no sign of the boys. No sound of their childish voices.

She traced the path they usually followed around to the front of the roadhouse. There were a couple of cars parked near the entrance, customers enjoying a glass of beer on a warm afternoon, Pop acting as host and barkeep. But no children. The school bus had come and gone without depositing her boys at their usual stop.

Anxiety twisted through her stomach. Last night Danny had been incredibly upset, but this morning he'd kissed her goodbye and gone off almost eagerly, with the promise that everything would be all right.

Whirling, her heart pounding, Sunny raced back toward the kitchen. She passed Dean, who called after her, "What's wrong?"

Nothing, she hoped. Sometimes the boys missed the bus because they were fooling around on the playground. Or Mrs. Tuttle forced them to stay after school for misbehaving. But they called! That was the only way they could get home if they didn't catch the bus. She had to drive down the hill and pick them up.

She snatched the phone from the hook. With trembling fingers, she punched in the school's number.

"Mount Wilson school. Mr. Durand speaking."

It's after hours, Sunny thought wildly. The school secretary was gone. So were all of the students.

"Mr. Durand, this is Sunny McCloud. My boys didn't come home on the bus this afternoon and I wondered if—"

"I've been meaning to call you, Ms. McCloud. I've been gone most of the day at a symposium, but I was very disturbed when I learned your twins were not at school today. Truancy is a very serious—"

"Not at school?" She nearly screamed the question. She'd sent her boys to the bus this morning at the usual hour, lunches in hand. How could they not have— "Why didn't someone call me?"

"Really, Ms. McCloud, we're running a school of seven hundred children here. A parent needs to take a certain amount of responsibility for the behavior of his or her children."

All the strength drained from her legs. Vaguely she was aware of Dean dragging a chair across the room, taking the phone from her hand and forcing her to sit down. He shoved her head between her knees. The dark curtain that had threatened lifted slightly, and she drew a deep breath. Her boys. Where were they?

Dean finished the conversation with the school principal. His questions were terse. Succinct. And troubled.

He hung up the phone and knelt in front of Sunny. "Sweetheart, I think the twins have run away."

"They could have been kidnapped." The mere thought shot terror into her soul.

"No, I don't think so. With Danny's problem—"

Pop burst into the kitchen. "Missy, I thought you bought us a whole carton of them chips and cheese munchies the last time you went shoppin'. For the life of me, I cain't find but a half a carton."

Sunny raised her gaze to meet Dean's. Instinctively her hand covered her mouth. Her sons would live on salty snacks if she'd let them. "Dear God, we've got to find the boys."

"THE SHOVEL'S GONE from the toolshed." Dean returned from his search of the immediate area around the roadhouse to find Quinn Petersen and his wife, Mindy, questioning Sunny about the boys. They were all sitting around one of the long tables in the dining room. Pop was there, too, silently wringing his hands and looking older and more frail than Dean had ever seen him.

Sunny glanced up at him. Her complexion was pale, her eyes red-rimmed. Deep in his gut, Dean felt every ounce of the pain she was experiencing.

"If the shovel's gone, that means they must be planning to search for gold." She shot Quinn a look. "Where would they go? You've been talking to them. Is there a specific place you've mentioned?" The desperation in her voice was a sure sign she was barely holding on to her composure.

The big man shrugged. "Any creek bed would be as good a guess as the next. Don't they realize the amounts of gold up here are minuscule?"

"They're just little boys." Her chin trembled. "How were they supposed to know that?"

Mindy took her hand. "It's okay, hon. The twins will probably show up on their own as soon as they get hungry."

Dean placed his hands on Sunny's shoulders to calm her and offer his support. Gently his thumbs kneaded the tense muscles that knotted across her back. "Mindy's right. And if they don't come back, we'll find 'em. They can't have gone far."

"Where's the sheriff? He should be here by now. It's been forever since I called. We need to put search parties together. It's almost dark. We can't leave them out there..." Her voice caught and she was unable to continue the thought.

"They're good boys, missy. You'll see..." Pop's voice dropped to a pained whisper, so weak Sunny had to wonder if he was experiencing another heart attack. Tears pooled in his eyes. "I should have known what they was up to."

"It's not your fault, Pop." If anyone was to blame, she was the guilty party. For not recognizing Danny's problem sooner. For not getting him help when he needed it.

The sound of an approaching car brought them all to their feet. They hurried outside to meet the sheriff.

"No sign of the boys yet?" he asked as he settled his cap squarely on his head.

"Not yet," Dean responded.

"Where are the search teams?" Sunny asked frantically. "Are they bringing dogs? What's taking them so long?"

"I'm sorry, Sunny," the sheriff said. "It's no more than half an hour till sunset and then we'll lose the light. There's not much we can do now."

"But you have to!"

"I've talked to Gene at the ski area. He's rounding up his search-and-rescue people. They'll be out and looking for your boys at first light tomorrow morning."

"No! You can't wait. My babies are all alone. There's a mountain lion on the loose. And...and that sniper! Anything could happen..."

She broke down then and Dean took her in his arms. He'd never known a woman could love so much, with such power that it was a physical thing, filled with warmth and determined strength. For the first time in his life, he envied anyone who was on the receiving end of that kind of passion.

Quinn and the sheriff stepped away a few feet, talking in low tones as they made plans for the morning search. Mindy hovered nearby, looking just as Dean felt, helpless to offer any real assistance. Finally she placed a reassuring arm around Pop.

When the sheriff drove away, Sunny lifted her head from Dean's chest. She'd left a damp mark on his shirt. Drawing a shuddering breath, she lifted her chin at a stubborn angle that mimicked Danny's gesture of determination not to be placed back in second grade.

"I'm not going to simply wait here," she announced. "I'm going to look for my boys."

"I'll go with you." It was an easy decision for Dean to make. Sunny and her sons were as important to him as anyone he'd ever known.

THEY SET OFF on the trail that Sunny knew was the most familiar to the boys. A trace of color still remained in the twilight sky, but within the forest itself darkness had already arrived and the air was chilly.

The beam of her flashlight skittered along the uneven path as she searched for signs that the twins had gone this way. She prayed for the sight of a crumpled potato-chip bag or a candy wrapper. At least she felt better and more under control now than she had earlier. She was actually *doing* something. Waiting had been impossibly difficult.

The light caught a movement ahead on the path. Sunny gasped as two golden eyes reflected back at her. Predator eyes that could see in the dark. Panic threatened as an image of a mountain lion on the prowl leaped into her mind.

"What is it?" Dean asked from behind her.

At the sound of his voice, the animal darted soundlessly into the trees—his profile low to the ground—and vanished within a few feet of the trail.

She drew an uneasy breath. "A fox, I think." Too small an animal to attack her boys, she thought in relief. Their prey was most often rodents and unwary squirrels, not towheaded little boys who were running away from home.

A mountain lion wouldn't be so discriminating, she realized with grim awareness.

"Maybe I ought to take the lead," Dean suggested.

"I know the way better than you do." Though she was grateful for Dean's company. He'd insisted they each carry a day pack of food and a water bottle, plus warm jackets and a first aid kit. She'd been so distraught, she probably would have gone off without any supplies. In contrast, Dean seemed completely in control of his emotions, issuing orders and making decisions in the same efficient way he must surely have practiced medicine.

But then, he didn't know they were searching for *his* children. Now seemed a poor time to tell him. At least one of them should remain calm and under control. Revelations about his paternity would simply have to wait.

She swallowed hard and gnawed on her lower lip. How would he react? she wondered. She quickly pushed the thought aside and focused on searching for the boys.

As the path angled upward her breathing became more labored. They were heading toward the fire lookout, she realized in dismay. The boys would know there wasn't any gold there. She should have aimed toward the lower elevations where winter creeks ran dry this time of year.

Dean brushed his hand against her arm. "Listen," he whispered.

She stopped and held her breath. Night sounds were elusive, their direction hard to pinpoint. But in the distance she thought she heard talking. A male voice muffled by the trees.

"Campers?" she asked as softly as she could. Or the sniper? she left unasked, the thought shivering silently though her body.

"I don't know. Let's see if we can find out."

He stepped in front of her and took the lead. Noiselessly he continued up the path. As they entered a clearing, he switched off his flashlight. Sunny did the same, letting the moonlight guide them until they reentered another stand of trees.

The clearly male voice was closer now and so was the fire lookout. It stood at the top of the hill, an ominous silhouette against the stars.

"Dean?"

"Shh." Gesturing for her to stay back, he moved forward even more cautiously.

From the lookout came the sudden boyish cry, "Hey, cut that out!"

"That's Howie!" Sunny would know her son's voice anywhere. She started to run toward the lookout.

Dean snagged her by the arm. "He's not alone, Sunny. We don't know who else is in there. Or what they're doing."

"Oh, Lord..." Her stomach churned. Who in the world could he be talking to? Myriad possibilities raced through her mind—none of them pleasant.

Edging closer to the lookout, they made their way around to the front of the boarded-up structure. How could anyone have gotten inside? she wondered. By now she could hear both of her boys talking. They were alive. For the moment, that knowledge buoyed her spirits.

Dean kept circling the building until he spotted a loose board along the foundation. He pried it open and peered underneath the lookout. A faint light outlined a trapdoor above.

"Wait here," he ordered.

"I'm going with you."

"We don't know who's inside."

"My sons are. That's all I need to know." She knew they could go back to the roadhouse and call for help. But they had surprise on their side. She was determined to get her sons back. Now.

They maneuvered into the close confines under the building. Finally Dean signaled he was ready.

He shoved at the trapdoor and burst upward. Sunny leaped up right behind him.

The boys screamed. The older male grunted as Dean slammed into him, and two bodies rolled across the floor, arms flailing. Sunny scooped the twins protectively into her embrace.

"Mom! What are you doing here?"

"Don't hurt Stevie."

"He didn't do anything wrong. Not on purpose."

"This is where he sleeps."

"That's why he tried to scare us off the other day."

"He didn't mean to shoot you, Mom."

"He feels real bad about the bird."

Everybody was shouting and yelling at the same time.

Dean's commanding voice silenced the twins. "It's okay, Sunny. I've got him under control."

Peering around the boys, the faint light of two candles allowed Sunny to see Dean had a young man fully subdued and in an arm lock. The youngster's eyes were wide with terror. A bad case of acne made his face look almost grotesque. His lank, dirty hair and the slight suggestion of a mustache added to the fearsome appearance.

Almost immediately, Sunny felt a rush of sympathy for the adolescent. He looked to be no more than fifteen. And from the pile of blankets in one corner of the room, and a few empty cans, it was apparent he lived here in the lookout.

"What's this all about?" she asked sternly. "This is Forest Service property."

"Lemme go," the boy demanded, trying to squirm away from Dean.

"Not until you talk to us, hotshot," Dean said.

Sunny slid her gaze around the room until it landed on a rifle propped in one corner. She gasped. "You're the sniper!"

"I was just messin' around," he said. "I didn't mean to hurt nobody."

"You've been shooting at people because you're *bored?* Where are earth are your parents? And why haven't they—"

"Mom!" Howie interrupted. "Stevie's mother told him he couldn't come home anymore 'cause he flunked out of school. He didn't have anyplace to go, so he's been hanging out here."

"He's like me and can't read any good," Danny said, tugging on her sleeve. "Mom, if I flunk out of school, are you gonna throw me out of the house, too?"

"Certainly not." Fiercely she pulled Danny into her arms, so grateful to have him safe and all in one piece. "Don't you ever think that. I've been trying to reach Mr. Durand all day to talk about getting you special tutoring instead of putting you back a grade. Or maybe shift you to a different teacher." One who had some knowledge and understanding of dyslexia and was willing to work with her son. "But no matter what happens at school, you're my son and I love you. I'd *never* send you away."

"And, young man," Dean said pointedly to Danny, "you and your brother put your mother through hell by running away. She's been scared to death. I think you both owe her an apology."

The two boys hung their heads, muttering, "Sorry, Mom."

Evidently Dean had eased his grip on Stevie because in a sudden move the teenager twisted away from him.

Before either Sunny or Dean could act, he had dropped down through the trapdoor and vanished.

"Dean, you have to go after him," Sunny insisted. "That boy can't be living up here on his own. His family needs to be horsewhipped and he needs a good lecture about using a gun carelessly. We have to let the authorities know what's happened."

"He's gone now, Sunny. I'd never find him in the dark." Dean picked up the rifle from the corner and slung it over his shoulder. "Right now, the most important thing is to get your two boys home. At least if Stevie doesn't have his weapon he won't be taking potshots at anyone. We'll let the sheriff know he's out here when we get back to the roadhouse."

Eager to get her sons home, Sunny reluctantly agreed. But she couldn't help feeling that if she was unable to help Danny with his learning disability, he might someday be so frustrated by failure that he would run away again. An adolescent would be a lot harder to locate than an eight-year-old boy.

Once back at the roadhouse, she called the sheriff to let him know the boys had been found, then fed the children and Dean a light dinner. Danny was so tired he almost drifted off to sleep before he could clean his plate. Finally she tucked the boys into bed and kissed them good-night.

Operating on the remnants of adrenaline, she prepared herself for bed, washing her face as she did every night, brushing her hair and slipping a cotton gown over her head.

It was only after she realized that the roadhouse was totally quiet and everyone else was asleep, that the reaction set in. She began to shake uncontrollably.

Her boys could have died out there! The sniper could have been some evil man, a murderer, not a lonely adolescent with acne. In the dark there were unseen hazards. Cliffs with precipitous drops. Mountain lions. Snakes.

The walls began to close in on her. She went downstairs and paced the length of the dark dining room. But nothing helped.

An instinct she couldn't identify drove her outside, to the back of the roadhouse. To where the stars still shone and the moon cast sensual shadows. To Dean's van.

He was standing beside the vehicle, his shirt unbuttoned and the snap on his jeans undone, as though he'd been preparing for bed and then had changed his mind. He'd decided to wait. For her. Because he'd known somehow she needed him.

When she sobbed his name, he opened his arms and she stepped into his embrace. It felt as if after a very long journey she had finally come home.

"Hold me, Dean. Just hold me. Please."

Kisses feathered her forehead. "For as long as you want."

"I got to thinking about... I was so scared. I didn't want to lose them. My babies."

"Shh, sweetheart. It's all right." He soothed his hands across her shoulders and down her back. She trembled like a butterfly in his arms. A frightened, fragile butterfly he wanted to protect. She was so tough, so strong, and at the same time enormously vulnerable.

"There's something... You need to know..." Her voice quavered.

"There's nothing I need to know except that you're here, with me."

"But—"

He halted her protest with a kiss. She tasted of sweet mountain nectar, like a honeybee who had visited sage and pine, wildflowers and cool pools of nature's pure artesian water. He drank his fill.

With a soft moan of surrender, she let her hands slide up his chest, across his bare flesh, and link behind his neck. She moved against him. The heat of her, her innate sensuousness set fire to his passion that he'd only marginally been keeping in check. He kneaded her scalp, her nape, the feminine swell of her hips, learning each delicate contour in an unforgettable tactile experience. Beneath the soft fabric of her gown, she was sleek and supple. Familiar and desirable.

He wanted her. Needed her.

"Sunny, come into the van with me." He covered her face with a dozen tender kisses. "I want to make love with you. I need you, baby, more than I've ever needed anyone in my life." It was true. He felt the urge so keenly, he knew there'd never been another woman like this. Never could be.

She shivered against him, making a small, hungry purr of acceptance.

The bed at the back of the van with its tumble of blankets was a generous size for one, but crowded for two. It didn't matter. He wanted them to be so close, a narrow cot would have been more than adequate.

As she helped him remove her short gown, he skimmed his palms over her rib cage and along the rounded side of her breasts. He delayed touching her more fully, first wanting to taste her sweet flavor again, teasing himself with the anticipation. Blood pulsed through his veins, hot and heavy.

"You are so beautiful," he whispered. He didn't need to see the fine grain of her skin, the rosy hue of her nipples, or the honey blond triangle that covered her mound to know how they would appear in full light. For him, darkness hid nothing. In his mind's eye he saw everything clearly. With his fingertips he mapped it all in intimate detail.

She arched up to him. "Dean..." Her voice caught on a sharp breath as he slid two fingers across her secret nub.

"I know. I can't seem to go slow."

"I don't want you to."

Her acceptance fanned the flames that were determined to consume him. He wrenched himself free long enough to rip off his shoes and jeans, finally releasing the painful pressure on his arousal.

Groaning, he lowered himself over her. "I don't want to hurt you." He took a nipple into his mouth to suckle the sweet flavor.

"You won't hurt me. I'm ready." She wrapped her arms around him and drew him toward her. This was where she belonged. With the man she loved. The man who had fathered her children. "So ready."

She opened to him without hesitation, welcoming him. She arched toward him with the full force of her longing. And he drove himself home, thrusting into her. She accepted his power and strength, every bit of his masculinity. Again and again.

On an explosive gasp, she cried his name and scored his back with her nails. She shattered like a bright shower of meteors across the midnight sky. In response, he gave a hoarse call of his own and she felt his surge of release filling both her body and her soul.

She drifted on a soft cloud of awareness. Bodies slick with perspiration touched skin to skin. Breathing slowed to a steady rhythm of sated pleasure. Hands caressed leisurely, kisses gentle and soothing. Soft words spoken without meaning. Chill air raised gooseflesh. Wrapped together in warm blankets, the weight of his arm across her chest was a welcome possession.

Finally she gave in to bone-deep weariness as sleep claimed her.

THE RAUCOUS CALL of an irritable blue jay woke her. For a moment she was disoriented, confused by the hard, muscular heat of the body next to her and the deep sense of satisfaction that filled her with a different kind of warmth.

Slowly she opened her eyes and discovered the first light of dawn was seeping into the van.

"Oh, my gosh!" She sat up abruptly.

With a groan, Dean rolled away. "What's wrong?" he mumbled.

"It's morning." She scrambled off the bed and snatched up her nightgown. "Pop always gets up early. If I don't get back inside—"

Catching her by the wrist, Dean said, "I'll have a morning kiss, Ms. McCloud. If you don't mind." Wide-awake now, his blue eyes sparked with sensual invitation.

"Dean, really, I can't. There's no time."

"Always time for a kiss." As he sat up to meet her halfway, the blanket slipped off the bed, and she got a full view of his beautiful masculine body. And his arousal.

"Dean . . ." she warned, suppressing her desire to climb back into bed with him.

He kissed her. Almost chastely. "I'll let you go. For now." Swinging his legs over the side of the bed, he picked up his jeans. "In fact, after breakfast, if it looks like everything is under control with the twins, can you and Pop manage on your own for a couple of hours?"

"Sure. Why?"

"If we're going to enjoy a repeat performance of last night—and I certainly hope we will—I need to visit a drugstore."

Frowning, she echoed, "Drugstore?"

Standing, he brushed strands of her sleep-mussed hair away from her face. "I didn't act very responsibly last night. It's my fault. I've wanted to make love with you from the first time I saw you dangling from the roof. I should have done a lot better job of planning ahead, but I didn't. *Next* time, I intend to have a whole box of condoms on hand."

She felt herself go pale, and her heart changed places with her stomach. "Of course. You're right." And she'd been incredibly foolish. Again.

"Honey, as much as I want you, I'm in no position to make any kind of a commitment. For all practical purposes, I'm an unemployed bum. This wouldn't be a good time for me to start a family. Unless, last night..."

The knot in her stomach tightened. She lifted her chin, fighting the pain and the burning threat of tears. "Don't give it a second thought, Dr. Weylin. If I'm pregnant—and I sincerely hope that I'm not—I promise I won't trouble you with the details."

Whirling, she slid open the van door and dashed toward the roadhouse. Dean Weylin hadn't wanted to be a father to her children nine years ago. Why should she expect his feelings to be any different now?

Chapter Nine

He'd made a strategic mistake.

Either that or the San Gabriel Mountains were about to experience an unseasonable cold snap for early November. Since Dean had told Sunny he was going shopping for condoms that morning, the temperature at the Cloud High Roadhouse had dropped to subzero. Frosty fury was evident in every biting word she spoke. Icicles nearly leaped at him from her angry eyes and she held herself so rigid, she might as well have been a snowman.

Dean wasn't entirely sure what had gone wrong. A man was supposed to be responsible about sex, wasn't he? Particularly when he cared about the woman.

Granted he'd gotten carried away last night and should have known better. But that slip shouldn't have sent her into a frigid blue funk.

Tunneling his fingers through his hair, he figured maybe Sunny wasn't actually mad at him. It could be that his reminder about responsible sex had triggered her residual anger at the man who had fathered her twins and then dumped her. Could be she was mad at *that* bum and not at Dean.

But he'd sure been on the receiving end of a major cold shoulder since he'd gotten back from his quick trip to town. And now he'd just been banished from Sunny's kitchen.

Spotting Danny sitting on a boulder well away from the roadhouse, Dean headed in that direction. Considering it wasn't a school day, the youngster looked particularly glum. He stared at his feet, fixating on his unlaced sneakers.

"Hey, tiger, what's happening?" Dean asked, hoping to cheer him up and lift his own mood at the same time.

The boy shrugged. "Nothin'."

"Yeah? From the way you look, I would have guessed the Dodgers just lost the World Series and you'd had a million bucks riding on them."

"The Dodgers aren't ever gonna make the series. They stink!"

"Oh." Dean picked a spot nearby and sat down, using a pine tree for a backrest. "So if you didn't just lose your shirt, what else could be so awful?"

"Mom's real mad at me."

"She was pretty upset yesterday when we realized you and your brother had run away. Women can get pretty emotional about a thing like that. But she'll get over it. You just have to give her a little time."

Danny raised his gaze. For an instant Dean thought he knew where he'd seen that incredible blue before, but the knowledge was fleeting, slipping away before he could fully grasp the memory. For the millionth time he cursed the gang-banger who had shot him and erased a large piece of his past.

"Are you and Mom gonna get married?"

The boy's question slammed into Dean's gut. "It's a little premature to be thinking about that sort of thing."

"How come? You like her, don't you?"

"Well, yeah, but there's a lot more to marriage than just liking a woman."

"Like what?"

Clearly Dean had never suspected how difficult it would be to answer an innocent child's questions. Of course, he didn't have a whole lot of experience with kids. "Among other things, a man needs to have a decent job and be able to support a woman properly before he even begins to think about marriage."

"So? You're a doctor. Isn't that a good job?"

He remembered that being a doctor left little time to have a relationship with anything except his stethoscope. Hardly a warm, intimate union, nothing like what he'd enjoyed with Sunny last night.

"I'm not a doctor anymore, Danny. In fact, until I can get my brain unscrambled, I'm not much good for any kind of job."

Lowering his gaze back to his thoroughly engrossing shoes, Danny said, "Maybe if I'd had a dad I wouldn't be so stupid."

"Oh, man—" Dean stood and reached out uncertainly, then went with his instincts. He hauled the kid into his arms. Shoot, he'd never had to deal with a thing like this. He wasn't sure he knew how. He only knew he didn't want to mess up. Danny McCloud was a real important little guy.

"Don't you ever believe that, kid. Not for a minute. If there's anybody who's stupid, it was the guy who walked out on your mom."

The screen door to the kitchen flew open and banged against the wall. Sunny screamed, "Dean! Come quick! There's a woman in here who's stopped breathing!"

Years of training kicked into high gear.

Dean lowered Danny to the ground, then raced for his van. He snatched his medical bag—unused for months—from under the seat and headed for the back of the roadhouse. A hundred possibilities raced through his mind that would account for breathing to stop. Trauma involving a crushed chest, maybe a fall or a car accident. Heart attack. A copycat sniper on the lose who was a far more accurate shot than the runaway adolescent.

Danny had beaten him to the back door and held open the screen for him. The kid's eyes were like big blue saucers.

"It's okay, son. We only have to do the very best we can. That's all anybody can ever ask of us."

Bursting into the dining room at a run, Dean found a crowd hovering around a young woman who was clearly unconscious. She'd been laid out on one of the tables, and a man who resembled Ichabod Crane had her nose pinched between his fingers and was rhythmically blowing into her mouth.

"What happened?" Dean snapped open his bag. Pulling out his stethoscope, he listened for the woman's heart sounds—weak and thready.

"We were hiking." Keeping up the breathing rhythm, Ichabod glanced up. "Bee sting. She's allergic." He blew into the woman's mouth, but her chest didn't respond by rising. "I thought I could get her down the hill. My wife—"

"You did the right thing." Dean said the encouraging words, as required for decency, but he knew the woman's throat was entirely closed due to the allergic reaction. She'd die if he didn't take action within the next few minutes.

"I want this room cleared," he ordered. "Pop, bring me the strongest bottle of whiskey you've got."

The woman's husband started to object.

Dean ignored him. "Sunny, I'll need clean sheets and towels. All you've got." He retrieved the tracheotomy kit from his bag, set it out and rinsed his hands with whiskey. "Have somebody call 911. Tell 'em a helicopter would be nice." To the husband, he said, "I've got her now. You did good."

"You're really a doctor, aren't you? I mean, you'll be able to—"

"Dr. Dean Weylin, University Hospital," he automatically replied.

From the corner of his eye, Dean spotted Danny and Howie both watching the proceedings in rapt attention. He should send them from the room along with rest of the onlookers, he thought, but remembering the incident with the injured bird, he let the impulse slide away. This wouldn't be a gruesome bit of surgery and he didn't think it would hurt the boys to observe a doctor at work.

Scalpel in hand, he tipped back the woman's head, exposing her neck. He poured the remaining whiskey across the slender column, aware her life rested in his hands. There wasn't anyone else within an hour's drive who could help. As he'd told Danny, he'd have to do the best he knew how.

By the time the woman was covered by a clean sheet, as protection against bacterial infection, it had all come back to him. The angled incision. A bright line of blood appearing, then the sight of the airway. The easy parting. Inserting the tube. The breathing sounds that meant the woman was drawing in life-giving oxygen. Color returning to her face. A relieved sigh from her husband.

Dean inhaled deeply, rotating his shoulders against the stress that had settled there. An easy bit of surgery, but a procedure he hadn't performed in more than a year. Good job! he told himself, his lips curling sightly. This was what being a doctor was all about—saving lives. He wondered how he could have possibly forgotten.

Feeling inordinately proud of himself, he shot a smile toward where the twins were standing.

In response, he got two sets of thumbs-up. It looked like they'd both have a story to relate for show-and-tell next week.

AFTER THE HELICOPTER landed in her parking lot and the patient was transported to Community Hospital, Sunny started to clean up her dining room. They'd had to close the roadhouse during the emergency and hadn't reopened yet. But that was all right. The experience of having someone almost die right in front of her eyes was terribly unsettling. She wondered how doctors managed life-and-death decisions on a day-to-day basis.

The recollection of Dean's competent, take-charge manner sent a ripple of apprehension down her spine. He was beginning to *remember* the medical training he'd forgotten.

What else would he remember about the past? she wondered, her throat closing around the thought as if she were allergic to the possibility. And how soon would those memories reappear?

She looked up from scrubbing the table as Dean came into the dining room. He'd changed his blood-spattered clothes and washed up. A sexy, confident smile played at the corners of his lips and his footsteps seemed particularly light.

Sunny would have liked nothing better than to wrap her arms around him and give him a congratulatory kiss for what he'd accomplished, for saving a life. Fear of ultimate rejection for both herself and her sons held her back.

"This place smells like a distillery," he said.

"One of my customers got a little sloppy with a bottle of whiskey." She dipped her rag into the bucket of soapy water and scrubbed the table.

"Good thing he did, too."

Forcing herself to appear nonchalant, she asked, "Do you think that woman will be all right?"

"I'd say the prognosis is excellent." He took her scrub rag from her hand and placed it on the table, effectively trapping Sunny between his rock-solid body and the table. Tension pulled tight between them. Memories thrummed like high-velocity wind across a power line—his recollections of last night, hers of the past. "What troubles me a lot more is how come you've been so mad at me all day. How 'bout we talk it out?"

She swallowed hard. "What is there to talk about? Last night when we made love it was a very enjoyable interlude—"

"Interlude?" He lifted his eyebrows and his eyes sparked with a lightning bolt of surprise.

"You made it quite clear from the start that you're here because you needed to rest and recover from your injuries. As soon as you're able, you're planning to go back to your medical training. Isn't that right?"

"You're making it sound like I'm interested in little more than a one-night stand. That isn't true."

"No? This morning it sounded like you weren't planning on becoming a family man anytime soon. And after seeing you save that woman's life, I'd say you're very nearly recovered."

He hesitated, his expression thoughtful. "I admit the neurological connections in my brain lined up as soon as I had that scalpel in my hand. And I actually think working with Danny and those plastic alphabet letters is helping me as much as it is him. But none of that means I'm entirely recovered. Not by a long shot."

Her heart sank with the realization that she'd guessed right. His recovery was well on its way. "So you're getting better, and pretty soon you'll go back to your old life. I'd just as soon not be left with a broken heart. That happened to me once and it wasn't a very pleasant experience." He'd been the culprit nine years ago. She'd be foolish to think for even an instant it wouldn't happen the same way again.

In spite of the Closed sign on the front door, a burly delivery man with massive arms and shoulders to match yanked the door open. He shoved a handcart filled with cases of beer inside.

"Hey, Sunny, heard you had some excitement up here." Without bothering to ask permission, he wheeled the load behind the bar.

"A little," she conceded. She tried to duck away from Dean but he blocked her escape.

"We aren't through talking yet, Sunny."

"Look, I have a business to run. I've got to get my checkbook and then make sure the order is right so I can pay Tonio. I don't have time—"

"I'll get your checkbook," he said grimly. "We're going to *make* time, Sunny. Just you and me."

Her eyes widened at the threat.

"Where's your checkbook?" he demanded.

"In the top drawer of my desk in the kitchen." Her tongue swept out to lick her lips and she shook her head, remembering. She'd been working on the books upstairs in the early morning hours before they'd taken Danny to the psychologist. She'd been trying to find money where none existed so that, if necessary, she could pay the doctor. "No, it's in my bedroom on my dresser. I left it there—"

"I'll be right back and then we're going to continue this discussion."

Dean left without letting her respond. She had this whole thing wrong, he realized. It wasn't that he didn't want a family. The timing was simply wrong. But later—

He stopped midway up the stairs. What did he want after he got his life back together? He'd been so wrapped up in his own recovery, he hadn't given any thought to his future. He certainly hadn't considered having a wife as part of that life, much less a couple of kids.

Continuing up the stairs, he decided he ought to begin thinking about that possibility pretty darn soon. Assuming he could figure out what the hell was really bothering Sunny.

Sunny's room was bright and airy, with a view out onto the highway and the hills beyond. But the scent of her was here. All around him, wreaking havoc with his senses. His throat went dry at the sight of her neatly made bed. She hadn't slept there last night. *She'd slept with him*. With raw, primitive need, he wanted her again. In her bed. Or his bed. Or out in the woods on a picnic blanket. It didn't matter where. A one-night stand wasn't going to be enough. He wouldn't settle for that.

The muscles of his groin pulled taut as he imagined having Sunny all to himself anytime he wanted, day or night. Mostly the nights, he mused, recalling how he'd slid into her welcoming heat, moved inside her and heard her soft moan of pleasure, all in the cocoon of darkness.

With a shake of his head, he pulled his thoughts away from the arousing image. He had a few matters to settle with Sunny before he could make that picture come true again.

He found the check register lying on Sunny's dresser. As he picked it up, a bottle of perfume tipped over. He righted it before anything could spill, and in the process his gaze was caught by a yellowed newspaper photograph with a brief caption.

He was the guy in the tux, a beautiful brunette on his arm. According to the date on the newspaper, the photo had been published nearly five years ago.

Now why the heck would Sunny have an old newspaper clipping of him attending one of his mother's charity shindigs?

Puzzled, he picked up the clipping, only to discover a more recent story beneath it—an article describing the emergency room shooting of Dr. H. Dean Weylin. Stunned, he turned it over. At the bottom of the small hoard of clippings lay a snapshot, another couple smiling back at him.

My God, he'd looked young then. The picture must have been taken close to ten years ago. And Sunny had looked—

A sharp stab of pain creased the inside of his skull, electrical currents connecting brain cells that had been silent and isolated since the shooting. That he had known Sunny before his recent arrival at the Cloud High Roadhouse was abundantly clear. Just how well he'd known her continued to elude him.

But his suspicions were aroused. He needed some straight answers and he wanted them now.

He flashed on conversations he'd had with the twins and the persistent feelings of déjà vu he'd experienced since he'd rescued Sunny from the rooftop.

As he stared into the mirror above Sunny's dresser, bright blue eyes glared back at him, eyes the identical shade as those that belonged to a pair of twins he'd only recently gotten to know. Coincidences like that just didn't happen.

He cursed his stupidity. How could he have been so blind?

A building sense of rage filled his gut. He'd been betrayed in the worst possible way.

HE KNEW.

The fury in his eyes would have told her even if Sunny hadn't noticed the newspaper clipping and telltale snapshot in his hand. She should never have sent him upstairs. After all the excitement, she simply hadn't been thinking clearly.

He shoved the check register at her. "Pay the man. Now."

Shaking from the inside out, she searched for a pen in the drawer behind the bar. Her signature was barely legible, her hand shook so badly. She slid the check across the counter to Tonio. "Thanks. I'll see you next week." Her voice sounded raspy, as if razor blades had been dragged through her throat.

Tonio parked himself on a bar stool. "This was my last delivery. I've got a little time. How 'bout a beer?"

"Bar's closed," Dean announced curtly. His fingers closed around Sunny's arm.

Her head snapped up. "Dean, I've lost enough business for today."

"Okay. Your choice." He leaned toward her, his whispered words cutting into her like the lash of a whip. "We can talk in private, or we can hang out all the dirty laundry in front of this guy. Which will it be?"

Easing himself off the bar stool, Tonio rose to his full six-foot-four height, all three hundred aggressive pounds of him. A loyal, oversize pit bull. "You got some problem with this bum, Sunny?"

"No." She called him off with a quick shake of her head. She'd desperately wanted to avoid this confrontation. But she couldn't involve anyone else in her troubles. "You'd better go."

Tonio looked doubtful. "You sure?"

"She's sure." Dean hustled her out of the bar and toward the back of the roadhouse.

"You rough her up, mister," Tonio shouted after them, "and you'll have to answer to me."

Dean grimaced. Hell, he'd never in his life even considered hitting a woman. He wasn't going to start now. But he was mad. Real mad.

Once outside, he ushered Sunny up the trail that led to the fire lookout. But they didn't go nearly that far. Little more than out of earshot of the roadhouse.

He halted in a small clearing. "You want to tell me about this?" He showed her the snapshot.

"You don't remember?"

"No. But I can sure as hell make some good guesses."

She swallowed back the tightness that filled her throat. However painful the outcome, she could no longer hide the truth. "When you were a med student you used to camp up here."

"Often?"

"Weekends, mostly. And during the summer when you got breaks."

"We knew each other pretty well?"

She closed her eyes. At the time she'd thought she'd found her other half, the perfect man who a woman dreams about but never expects to find. "Yes."

"The twins?"

She knew what he was asking but the words wouldn't come. Her fears ran too deep, her insecurities still as paralyzing as those she'd endured nine years ago.

"Dammit, Sunny!" Firmly he grabbed her shoulders. "Are Danny and Howie my sons?"

To protect herself and her sons, she wanted to deny the possibility. But she couldn't. Slowly she nodded her head.

With a groan, he released her. "You had my kids and never even told me?"

"I tried."

He barked a mirthless laugh. "Sweetheart, if you'd told me, those boys would have known I was their father. I never would have walked away from that responsibility."

"That's what you say now. Nine years ago it was different."

"How so? I haven't changed that much."

If only that were true. "When I broached the subject of children, you very clearly informed me, and I quote, 'Becoming a doctor requires a major commitment. To dilute that effort by starting a family prematurely can destroy a med student and ruin his career.'" Those exact words had been seared into her memory and she'd played them back as if they were a constantly looping segment of audiotape.

His forehead furrowed. "Those are my father's words, not mine."

"He didn't say them to me. *You* did. I never even met your father. *Or* your brother, until recently. I was your dark little secret up here in the mountains, your recreational activity to wile away what few leisure hours you had." Foolishly, at the time she'd thought that was enough. She'd been willing to wait until he finished school. Until he was ready to start a family. But reality had interfered with that pipe dream.

"I don't believe you."

"No? Well listen to this. After you had waxed on about your commitment to your career, you informed me your father would stop paying your tuition if you had children, or even got married, before you'd finished your training." Unwelcome tears burned at the back of her eyes and she blinked them away. "Whenever you talked about being a doctor, you absolutely glowed, Dean. You were so determined. It was what you'd wanted since you were just a little boy. What was I supposed to do? Tell you about my pregnancy and know that through some misguided sense of obligation you'd destroy your entire future?" And probably destroy her love in the process.

He speared his fingers through his hair, creating even more disarray among the cowlicks. "The point is, you never gave me a chance to make that decision. Even after the twins were born, you cut me out."

"Funny, that's not how I saw it. After that day when I tried to tell you I was pregnant, you never came back. Not once. I grew fat and ugly, and if you'd dropped by even once in that whole nine months it would have been obvious I was pregnant with your babies." A single tear spilled down her cheek. Angrily she swiped at it with the back of her hand. "I may not have actually said the words, but you knew, dammit! You *knew* and you walked away."

Chapter Ten

Dean paced across the clearing and slammed his fist against a tree trunk. It stung like hell clear up to his shoulder. But it didn't help him remember what had really happened nine years ago.

How could he have abandoned Sunny if he had known, or even guessed, she was pregnant? He'd never been that callous. Certainly not about a woman he'd been sleeping with.

Damn! Why couldn't he remember?

Bits and pieces of the past had been coming back to him ever since he'd come up to the mountains. After performing the surgical procedure that afternoon, he'd begun to feel it would all come back. Every last shred of knowledge he'd gained, every experience that had touched his life in the past thirty-two years.

But there was still a big gaping hole in his memory, and Sunny was standing right smack in the middle of it. Along with his kids.

His rage and frustration threatening to boil over, he turned to Sunny. Her arms were folded protectively across her belly, her shoulders squared as if she expected him to throw the next punch at her midsection instead of a tree. She acted as if she was ready to stand up to him, but it was all bravado. He knew that. She was vulnerable as hell and he didn't want to think about that.

Along with the hole in his memory, she'd also left him with a huge void in his life. He'd realized when he woke from his coma that if he had died, damn few people would have missed him. It had been a very disconcerting feeling, one that still had the power to shake him.

But he had kids he'd never even known about. His progeny—children to whom he could pass on whatever wisdom he'd gained in life. He should have been a part of their lives, dammit! And they should have been a part of his.

"What you've done," he said grimly, "is unforgivable. For all practical purposes, you kidnapped my children."

Even in the deep shade of the pine forest, he could see she'd turned ashen. "That's not so. You didn't want them."

"If you were so sure of that, why didn't you bother to confirm your suspicions?"

"I didn't want you to feel obligated."

"And for the same reason, you kept silent until I found out for myself? If you weren't really trying to shanghai my kids, why didn't you just tell me the truth that first day when I hauled you off the roof?"

She lifted her chin. "In case you've forgotten, Dr. Weylin, you had no recollection of me at all that day. As far as you were concerned, I was a total stranger. One you instantly had the hots for, if I'm any judge of what I saw in your eyes. Just what would you have thought if I'd blithely announced you had two sons you'd never even heard about?"

That slowed him down for a moment. She'd certainly been right that he'd been hot for her. In spite of the way she'd obviously betrayed him, he still was. And that galled the heck out of him. "I would have thought you were a candidate for the psycho ward."

"But you don't think I'm crazy now?"

"I'm not going to deny my paternity, if that's what you're asking. In fact, I want Danny and Howie. I want to make up for all the time we've missed together. I want them to know I'm their father and I want them to know it now. And if you're not going to tell them, I will."

"No!" she whispered in panicky refusal. "Please don't. You can't just drop that kind of a bombshell on them."

"Why the hell can't I? It's true, isn't it?"

"Danny is at a very vulnerable point in his life. You can't simply waltz in—"

"Danny is just the point. The kid thinks the reason he can't read is because he never had a father. You did that to him, Sunny. You made him feel like he wasn't good enough to have a dad."

She shook her head, guilt washing over her, driven in dark waves by Dean's fury. "You don't understand."

"No, I don't."

"Maybe I should have told you, but it was you who never came back."

"A phone call would have been nice. How hard could that have been?"

"I did what I thought was best. For all of us. I never asked anything of you, Dean. Give me a little credit for that."

"You stole my kids. These days a father has rights. I intend to exercise mine."

Turning away, he headed down the path toward the roadhouse. Frantically Sunny grabbed his arm. "No! I won't let you do this. You've got to give me some time to prepare the boys."

Shrugging her off, he kept going. "You've had eight years."

"Then how much could a few more days hurt? You can't know for sure how this will affect them. If we're not careful, they could end up hating both of us. I don't want that, Dean." When his footsteps slowed, she said a silent prayer she would be able to reason with him. "Once you and I cared about each other. At least I cared about you. I don't want the twins to think there was anything ugly or nasty about the way they were conceived or why I never told them who you were. Even if you think I made the wrong decision nine years ago, wouldn't it be better if we did this together?"

He jammed his hands into his pockets and stared down toward the roadhouse.

"Please, Dean. We both have to think of the twins' best interests. Don't lose sight of that."

Releasing an audible sigh, he nodded. "All right, I agree. For their sakes, we should tell the boys together. But I insist it be soon. Too many years have already been lost."

"After we tell them..." Her voice quavered. "What are you going to do?" *Are you going to try to take my boys away from me?* The question she was too afraid to ask screamed through her mind. God knew she didn't want to do battle with this man, but she'd fight like hell for her sons. No one, absolutely *no one,* would take them away from her.

He hesitated. Too long, she thought, for the answer to be any of the words she might have hoped to hear.

"I don't know, Sunny." His voice was low and raspy, taut with emotion barely held in check. "This is all so new I haven't thought that far ahead yet."

As THEY RETURNED to the roadhouse, Sunny frantically searched for ways to delay the inevitable. Like a persistent rash, Dean wasn't going to go away until she actually did something about it. Then he might leave and take the boys with him. Given his cold anger toward her, the very best she could hope for would be a joint custody arrangement. Worst case, he would publicly accuse her of kidnapping and demand full custody. With his family's backing, he'd be able to hire the finest lawyers in town to press his case.

She doubted she had enough money to cover the charges for talking to an attorney's receptionist.

While they'd been gone, Pop had evidently re-opened the restaurant. He was scurrying around the kitchen slapping hamburger patties onto the grill and setting up serving trays.

"Here, I'll do that, Pop," Sunny offered. She took the spatula from him and turned the meat that was already cooking.

"We're getting ourselfs a passel of customers out there. Seems like Dean made the news, what with him saving that woman 'n all. Them two folks was soap oprey stars. Cloud High is gonna be famous, thanks to your young fella." Pop beamed her a smile. "Might be we could even pay off the roof if this keeps up."

Better yet, Sunny had gotten the reprieve she'd hoped for, though she knew it wouldn't last long.

Without looking at Dean to check his reaction to the situation, she said, "You go on back to the bar, Pop. I'll manage here."

"'Specks Dean better put on his best waitering out-fit. Them folks'll be looking fer a real celebrity out there. Maybe even want your John Hancock on a menu or two."

"I'll be there in a minute."

After Pop left, Dean came up to stand behind Sunny. She knew he was there. She could feel the heat of his gaze on her back. Less than twenty-four hours ago that warmth had been generated by high-level sexual tension. Now the impetus was anger. She nearly wept at the difference.

"This doesn't change anything, Sunny. We're still going to talk to the twins."

"We will. I give you my word."

"At this point, I'm not all that sure how good your word is."

She whirled to face him. "If we're talking honesty here, maybe you'd better search your conscience a little more deeply. Maybe you're hiding behind your amnesia so you won't have to face the truth about yourself. You didn't want me to have your baby so you decided to ignore the possibility. Maybe running away when things get tough is a genetic trait Danny picked up from you."

Without warning, he placed his hands on her shoulders, capturing her as though he wanted to kiss her—or throttle her. She could feel the controlled press of his fingertips, the heat of his palms, a vague sense of indecision. His blue eyes sparked with fury, not unlike the way they had once shone with desire.

Despite the conflicting emotions swirling between them, she reacted to his touch. A shocking sense of need shimmered along the surface of her flesh and curled toward her midsection. Even though at this moment he hated her and could potentially take her children away, he could still turn her on with the slightest touch. The knowledge made her breasts swell and her nipples pucker. Other, more intimate places received the same message of arousal.

It had always been this way with Dean. She was helpless to prevent her elemental reaction to the man she had once so eagerly loved. And still wanted with the same foolhardy need.

He pulled his hands away as if the heat she'd been feeling had burned him as well. A muscle ticked at his jaw.

"We'll talk later," he said roughly. He never should have touched her that way. It brought back every memory of the night they'd spent together. He'd kissed her along the velvety smoothness of her neck. Had tasted her, hot and sweet, and buried his face in the silken strands of her hair. And he wanted to do it all over again.

Damn her! She couldn't be right. He *never* turned his back on his responsibilities, no matter how tough the going got. A Weylin didn't do that. His father had drummed that into his skull for as long as he could remember. And so had his grandfather.

But the senior Weylins had made it entirely clear that a Weylin's responsibility led him toward med school, a successful surgical practice and eventually a position as Chief of Staff at University Hospital. That's what was expected of him. A careless moment, which might cause an unintended pregnancy— with all the potential complications such as an unsuitable marriage—would create an unacceptable detour from which a youthful Weylin might never recover.

As he pushed out through the door into the dining room, he began to sweat. The small voice of his conscience goaded him with the possibility that Sunny had touched on a truth he wasn't eager to hear.

"Hey, Dean! Where ya been?" All grins, Danny came running up to him. "Everybody's talkin' about you. Wow! Was that neat! Cutting right into that lady's throat. Man, Pete's dad never did anything like that," he chortled. "Wait till I tell him."

Dean cupped the back of the boy's head, all sweaty from play. A great rush of emotion brought tears to his eyes. *His son.* My God, he'd never realized what it would feel like. Elation filled his chest. Pride and awe warred in equal parts, and he wanted to shout from the top of Mount Wilson. *I have a son! Two of them!*

Pulling Danny hard against him, he hugged the boy fiercely.

"Hey, you're squishing me," Danny complained.

"Darn right I am." Dean laughed. "You're worth a thousand, zillion squishes. And so is Howie."

Pulling away, Danny looked at Dean as if he had grown a second head. "Are you okay?"

"I've never been better." Who would have guessed it would be such a spectacular feeling to know you'd fathered a kid? And double that pleasure with twins!

The racket of customers waiting to order—and Pop's frantic signals—finally caught Dean's attention.

Grinning foolishly, he picked a table of six to serve first. "What will it be, folks?" *You see those two good-lookin' twins over there? They're my sons. Pretty terrific, eh?*

Somehow he managed to get everyone's order, though he had to ask one guy three times before he got it straight. It didn't matter. He was a *dad*. Images of Little League games, fishing trips in the Sierras for the three of them, and loaning the car to the twins for prom night popped into his head. He frowned. The boys had better not put a single scratch on his car!

Returning to the kitchen to place the order, he came to a sudden halt. His gaze slid to Sunny's midsection—her narrow waist, her slim hips and the slender width of her pelvis. He pictured her full and rounded by pregnancy, the twins growing within her. A miracle of life.

"What are you looking at?" she asked.

His newfound sense of awe kicked up a level. "You had my babies."

"I'm aware of that."

"Thank you."

She cocked her head. "What are you talking about?"

"You could have made a different choice."

"No." She quickly denied the possibility. "I never considered any other option."

Propelled by a need to touch her, he walked across the room. He didn't know where his relationship with Sunny stood now. For the moment, all he could think about was that she had given birth to his children.

Sunny took a step backward but then decided to hold her ground. Slowly he placed his palm against the plane of her belly. She felt the heat of his hand through her jeans and the warmth spread in all directions, weighting her breasts and flowing to the apex of her thighs. He had the strangest look on his face, as though he'd discovered a cure for cancer—or won the lottery.

His hand moved back and forth, creating a wonderful burning sensation that swirled from the inside out.

"Dean?" she gasped. She shouldn't be letting him do this to her. Not here in her kitchen. Not at all, after the terrible things he'd said. Not when he might try to take the boys away from her. But she couldn't think straight. All she wanted was more.

"No matter what you thought at the time, I can't imagine you were ever fat and ugly."

A warm, achy shudder traveled through her body. "I was as big as the proverbial house. For the last two months, I couldn't see my toes."

"Was the delivery terrible?"

"I've had days that were more fun. But when it was over, I knew all the pain had been worth it." She'd held those two precious bundles in her arms and known she'd never felt such joy. Or been more alone.

He closed his eyes and when he opened them again, he smiled. "Thanks."

"Is that why you came into the kitchen? To find out how the delivery went?"

"I don't think so."

"Dean, have you been nipping at Pop's private reserve whiskey?"

He looked affronted. "Why do you ask that?"

"Because you've got a sappy expression on your face."

"I know. Must be an occupational hazard that comes from being a dad."

"My occupation is running a restaurant. It seems to me, Pop said there were customers waiting?"

"Oh, yeah. I forgot." His forehead furrowed, but the action did little to subdue his smile. "Two burgers, both with fries. One soft taco, no rice. A BLT and a tostada. And one cherry pie. I wrote it all down for you." Proudly he handed over the order ticket.

She checked it in surprise. With one small exception, he'd written every word correctly. Sunny realized he might not remember her yet, and the love she thought they had shared together, but the rest of his memories were swiftly returning. She told herself to be jubilant for his recovery. But in her heart, she felt the dull threat that he would soon leave her again.

She thought Dean would go back to the dining room then to see to the customers. Instead he brushed the back of his hand against her cheek. His eyes were a clear, brilliant blue, his smile touched with pure masculine swagger. Lord, it was as if he was the first man in the entire history of mankind who had ever managed to get a woman pregnant, thereby magically becoming a father.

"We'll work something out with the boys, Sunny. I promise you that. They're the most important thing that's ever happened to me."

She nearly cried. As much as she loved the twins, she wished that she rated a little higher on Dean's scale of notable people. "They're my whole life," she whispered.

"I want my folks to meet them as soon as possible."

She blanched. "If they see the boys, they'll instantly recognize—"

"I'll talk to Dad and explain the situation. He and Mother can start getting acquainted with Danny and Howie. Then, when we're ready to tell the boys they have a father, they'll already know their grandparents."

"I don't know, Dean. Often-told secrets don't stay secrets for very long. They might say something—"

"They have a right, Sunny. And so do I. I'll try to arrange something for this weekend."

"So soon?"

"Don't you agree the meeting is actually long overdue?"

Slowly she nodded. She really had little choice in the matter. The twins were Dean's children, too.

HE LOVED THE SMELL of a hospital.

The tangy scent of antiseptic mixing with the more pungent medicinal aromas, combined with the sound of doctors being paged over the loudspeaker system, reminded Dean of all the times he'd visited the hospital with his father. As a kid he'd tagged along on rounds, staying inconspicuously in the background. Or he'd hung out in the doctors' lounge listening to residents complain about long hours and low pay.

With his father's approval, he'd explored every area of the hospital. He knew the back way into radiology and where the staff kept a stash of candy in the physical-therapy section. By age fifteen he was a student volunteer, wheeling patients to occupational therapy sessions and delivering specimens to the labs. He'd done paperwork in the emergency room and taken special note of those private places where doctors would lure nurses if they wanted a quick kiss.

Striding across the lobby, Dean smiled to himself. Every night at dinner his dad had questioned him about what he'd learned at the hospital. There'd never been any doubt that Dean would eventually be a doctor, and his medical training had started young.

He could hardly wait to bring his sons here. He wanted them to love it, too.

Thank goodness when Dean and Sunny had met with the school principal yesterday he had agreed, after listening to their rationale, to keep Danny in the third grade. The school would pull him out of class for extra tutoring every morning, but for most of the day the boys would be together and Danny would avoid the stigma of being put back a grade. Combined with lots of extra help at home, Dean figured Danny's academic success would show marked improvement.

Reaching the bank of elevators, he tapped the Up button.

A nurse joined him to wait by the door. "Hello, Dr. Weylin. Good to see you. Are you planning to come back to work soon?"

A young woman with dark hair and doe eyes, she looked vaguely familiar but he couldn't come up with a name. "I hope to be back for the next rotation."

"That's wonderful. I'm sure the staff will be very pleased to hear that. You're one of the few residents who never yelled at the nurses." She glanced away shyly. "At least, you never yelled at me."

"Really? I guess I'll have to work at maintaining my reputation then."

A slight blush colored her cheeks as she stepped into the elevator. Dean had the feeling he might have flirted with her in the past. But he couldn't remember and now he didn't have any interest. In some strange way, even if Sunny had deceived him about the twins, she'd also spoiled him for any other woman.

The nurse exited the elevator at the fourth floor, giving him an encouraging smile as she said she'd look forward to his return to work, and Dean rode alone to the sixth-floor administrative offices.

His father's secretary waved him into the inner sanctum.

"Hello, son. Good to see you." Rising from his chair, Harrington Weylin extended his hand. At sixty-five, his erect figure was still as trim as it had been when he was in med school, and his hair had only recently begun to thin and show signs of gray among the blond. "Your mother has been missing you."

"I needed to get away, sir."

"I understand that." He gestured for Dean to sit in one of the leather chairs in front of his massive desk.

"But we'll both be glad to have you back anytime you're ready."

"Yes, sir."

"How are your, ah, studies going?"

Since the shooting, his father had been reluctant to concede that Dean had suffered a severe memory loss which might have meant he could never again practice medicine. He'd looked at the incident as simply another challenge a Weylin was asked to meet.

"Things are improving every day, Father. I think I'm going to be ready for the next rotation."

Relief washed over Harrington's face and he sat down. "I knew you could do it, son, in spite of what that gang-banger tried to do to you. Practicing medicine is as natural as breathing for us Weylins."

Dean had heard that comment often over the years, frequently while sitting right here in this same leather chair. He'd accepted it as true. In contrast, his brother, Rick, had chosen a different course. His father still viewed Rick's decision as a sign of rebellion.

"I met someone while up in the mountains. Someone I used to know."

"Oh?" Harrington tented his fingers together. "May I assume this someone is a woman?"

"Yes, sir. Do you remember when I was in med school I used to go camping up on Angeles Crest Highway?" Of course, Dean didn't recall that time in his life but thought his father might.

"I remember one summer you seemed particularly restless, and I was worried you were considering dropping out of school. It happens at some point to most med students. Even I had a few moments when my commitment weakened." He smiled proudly. "But I had complete confidence you'd come to your senses just as I had."

"I suppose it's not that unusual to question your career decisions." After meeting Sunny, had he struggled with what his future ought to be? Dean wondered. And had medicine won out over a woman he'd loved? Damn, why was the past still a blur?

"Originally I met this same woman that summer," Dean said. "She and her grandfather run a small roadhouse near the campground. At the time, she was about eighteen or nineteen. Evidently we got pretty close."

Harrington raised his eyebrows. "Just how close?"

That sappy smile Sunny had been teasing him about curled his lips. "She got pregnant, Father. I have two sons. They're eight-year-old twins—Danny and Howie."

Instead of looking pleased, Harrington scowled. "Now, son, you have to be wary of paternity claims. Some women want to take advantage of a man whom they know comes from wealth when all they're really looking for is a meal ticket. Blood tests will show—"

"They're my kids, Father. They've got Weylin written all over their faces." And in their blue eyes, which he'd been too stupid to recognize.

"Yes, well..." He shoved back from his desk, stood and paced across to the window. The hazy skyline of Los Angeles filled the view. "Perhaps she'll take a lump sum payment and be done with it. If not, I'm sure our attorneys can work out a reasonable support arrangement.''

Stunned by his father's reaction, Dean came to his feet. ''Dad, these are your grandchildren we're talking about, *my* sons, not some homeless kids off the street. You've gotta meet them. Why, Danny's likely to be the next Weylin doctor. He's already tried to repair a bird's broken wing. And Howie's so smart it scares me.'' In fact, when he thought about it, being a father was a scary proposition.

Harrington swung around to face his son. ''You say these boys want to be doctors?''

''I don't know about that exactly. We haven't talked about it yet. And Danny's got some academic problems. He has just been diagnosed as dyslexic, but I'm not worried now that he's going to be getting some help.'' And why should it matter what career the twins chose? ''The boys are great, Dad. You'll love 'em. So will Mother.''

With a surprising amount of reluctance, Harrington agreed Dean could bring the twins to visit the following weekend. Regarding the news that the boys didn't know Dean was their father yet, Harrington was equally cool.

''That may be just as well, son,'' he said. ''It's possible you may decide to let sleeping dogs lie, as they say. Remember, you haven't finished your residency yet. Considering you're still recovering from your injuries, this is hardly an ideal time for you to take on parental responsibilities.''

Dean's smile dissolved into a grim line. ''You're right, Dad. I'm about eight years late.''

Chapter Eleven

"What was it like when we were together?"

Dean's question jolted Sunny. He'd found her out-side wiping the umbrella table that sat in front of the roadhouse. It was midmorning, and the twins were at school and Pop was somewhere upstairs. The high-way was an empty black ribbon of asphalt. For most of the week since he'd discovered he was the father of her twins, Sunny had managed to avoid being alone with him. But this time he'd caught her off guard.

"What do you mean?" she asked.

"I thought if you told me where we went together, what we talked about, maybe it would jog my brain into remembering something."

Memories crowded in on her, nearly stealing her breath. The first time he'd kissed her. How they'd laughed at the antics of two squirrels fighting over a single pinecone when there were dozens on the ground. The eager way they had made love together. The in-credible journey of discovery that had left them both breathless. Thousands of images she couldn't possibly put into words.

She squeezed the damp cleaning rag hard enough so that she wouldn't remember the tactile feel of his flesh beneath her exploring hands. But, of course, it didn't do any good. She'd never forgotten what it had been like to touch him and be caressed in return. More recently, she had renewed each one of those erotic recollections as they had made love in his van.

"We didn't actually date much," she said, futilely trying to suppress the very memories he was asking her to recall. "I had to help Pop run the roadhouse. It was hard to get away for long periods of time."

"Didn't I even take you out to dinner?"

"Once. To Chez Fontaine's."

His lips slid into a sheepish grin. "My folks' favorite restaurant. I must have taken you there to impress you."

"You succeeded." But it was the details of what had happened after their meal, when he had taken her back to his apartment, that she remembered with far greater clarity.

"Did we go to the movies?"

"No. I usually had to work in the evenings, and you were up here to get a break from the city." She swiped halfheartedly at a spot on the table and wished she could as easily wipe away her memories. Recalling the past meant she had to face what she had lost. Or never truly had. "Sometimes if business was slow, we'd go sit out back and count the stars. You seemed to know all of the constellations that I'd never heard about."

He'd also known ways to touch her that she'd never dreamed about.

"Doesn't sound to me like I did a very good job of courting you."

"I don't recall complaining."

"Was the chemistry between us then like it is now? So hot we couldn't stop wanting each other."

Her head snapped up. He was looking at her in a studied way, his eyes narrowed. He took a step closer until his face was only inches from hers. His gaze settled on her lips, his eyes so dark and filled with desire, it left her speechless. If only it was love, not simply lust she saw burning there.

"I seem to remember I had a pickup truck with a small camper on the back," he said slowly, thoughtfully. "Did we make love there?"

He was standing so close, she couldn't breathe without catching his scent—spicy and masculine musk. She could hardly breathe at all, her throat was so filled with the past. "Yes."

His forehead furrowed. "Where else did we make love?"

"At your apartment." Her legs were weak from the memories and the wanting that was still so near the surface. "Once. That night after Chez Fontaine's."

"There were other places? Other times?"

The cool morning air shuddered through her. "Look, I can't do this, Dean. If you want to get your kicks by talking about all the places we made love, fine. But you'll have to do it on your own."

"I can't!" His jaw tightened. "I can't remember a damn thing about us and I want to. I want to know why I went off and left you. And why the hell you didn't tell me you were pregnant. Is that so hard to understand? I've lost a big chunk of my past and you're the only one who can fill in the blanks."

The need in his eyes, the stark helplessness, defeated her. "All right! There's a secluded spot about a mile from here. We used to take a blanket and a picnic lunch, only we usually forgot to eat. Once we made love in the front seat of your truck, or we tried to. I hit the damn horn with my butt, and we got to laughing so hard we couldn't do anything. And once we..." Her chin started quivering and she choked on a sob. "Telling you like this makes it sound so crass. So dirty. It wasn't like that, Dean. Every time it was beautiful." Tears spilled down her cheeks.

Swearing softly, Dean pulled her into his arms. She came willingly enough, and he tucked her head under his chin. He had the tantalizing feeling she'd always fit this perfectly, even their breathing synchronized when they were close. But he couldn't quite grasp the memory. It was like looking through a shattered windowpane, where all the images fractured into disjointed bits and pieces, none of which made sense.

She sniffed and he felt her body relax against him, softening in a very feminine way. "About the only other place you took me—besides that one nice dinner—was to Magic Mountain."

"Ah, I thought I remembered—"

"You got sick on everything that resembled a roller coaster."

He went very still. His brow furrowed. "You mean, when we went to Magic Mountain and the boys wanted to ride Colossus you knew I'd get sick?"

"Well, I thought maybe your head injury might have changed things. And you didn't have any objection to taking us there." Eyes still a little watery, she gave him a sly grin. "Besides, every woman deserves a few minutes of revenge on a guy who dumped her."

He choked and tried to keep himself under control. But the laugh started somewhere in his gut and he was helpless to prevent the outburst. It built until it was a roar that frightened two sparrows who had been searching the ground for crumbs near the table. "I'll get you for that, Sunny McCloud," he chortled. "One way or another, I'll get you." Soon, he hoped. Maybe even this weekend.

"HEY, MOM, watch me!" Howie did a cannonball off the diving board into the Weylin pool, spraying water over Dean, who was staying close by in case anything went wrong.

"Look at me, too!" Danny shouted. Water dripped and puddled at his feet as he mounted the diving board to repeat the process that had been going on since they'd arrived at the Weylin estate an hour or more ago. The three-story house and manicured grounds could hardly be called a home. Not in any lexicon Sunny was familiar with. It was simply too big, far too impressive to relate to anything she had ever known as a place where children grew up and become persons in their own right.

"Wait till Howie is out of the way," Sunny warned, her feeling of discomfort magnified by the ostentatious signs of wealth all around her.

Danny's splash rocked the bright blue inner tubes that were floating in the shallow end of the pool, a pool that came close to rivaling an Olympic venue in size.

Alice Weylin refilled Sunny's glass of ice tea. "Your sons are charming."

"Thank you," she murmured. Though Dean's mother had been cordial, Sunny couldn't remember a time when she'd felt so out of place. His mother was the epitome of old wealth, her hair beautifully coiffed, her figure tanned and massaged to perfection, the evidence of her face-lifts barely visible. Sunny—raised at a roadhouse in the mountains, who had a checkbook that regularly teetered on the brink of disaster—didn't belong here, and both Alice Weylin and she knew it.

"The boys certainly remind me of Dean and his brother, Rick, at that age. The resemblance is uncanny."

"Yes. The Weylin genes appear to run true."

"Of course, their existence was a bit of a shock to both Harrington and me. We hadn't even known about you, my dear. But then, I gather yours was a rather brief relationship."

Hearing a disapproving tone, Sunny dragged her gaze away from the activities in the pool and shot Mrs.

Weylin a look. "It was most of a summer." *I fell in love. How much time does that take?*

Without meeting Sunny's eyes, Alice asked, "Have you and Dean discussed custody arrangements?"

Fear tightened in her throat. "Not yet."

"Ms. McCloud, my husband has a great deal of influence in this community. He has served on a special task force for the mayor and is quite active politically. These days one has to be active if you want your business to succeed. And University Hospital is not only Harrington's business, it's his own personal kingdom." She turned and studied Sunny with care. In her pale eyes, there appeared to be a touch of sympathy. "Harrington likes the idea of an heir to the throne being available should the existing heir fail to measure up."

Sunny blanched at the warning.

"When I was married," Mrs. Weylin continued, "the wedding vows contained the bride's promise to obey her husband. When it came to the upbringing of my sons, I may have taken that vow too literally, and now it's far too late to change the rules of the game. Fortunately your generation is wiser than mine."

Their eyes met and Sunny recognized an ally in Mrs. Weylin, though not necessarily one who would challenge her husband directly. But she did love her sons, both of them. And perhaps she could learn to love her grandsons as well.

As Sunny was considering the implications of Mrs. Weylin's words, Howie came running up to them.

"Hey, Mom, isn't it great? Dean says we can come here anytime we want." He was bubbling over with enthusiasm even as his healthy, young body shivered in the cooling afternoon air.

"Yes, dear, that's wonderful." She wrapped a towel around him. How on earth would she ever compete if Dean and his father decided to claim custody rights, with or without Mrs. Weylin's approval? The twins would surely be tempted by the Weylin wealth and all the perks that would come with status and money. And so might a judicial court. She'd have nothing but her unbounded mother's love to offer as an alternative. The choice would be too difficult for the children, since they'd always been told "no" whenever it came to spending money on things they desperately wanted and she had to deny them.

Tears pressed at the back of eyes. She never should have agreed to bring her children here; she never should have admitted Dean was their father.

Nothing in her entire life meant more to Sunny than her sons. She would give her soul for them. Against all odds, she would fight *anyone* who tried to take them away from her.

"Danny 'n me are gonna play Ping-Pong, Mom. Is that okay?"

"If it's all right with Dr. Weylin," Sunny assured her son, who hadn't bothered to actually wait for her approval before he ran off.

"Harrington is a master at tempting others to do what he wants," Alice Weylin said a little sadly. "And then, when you've surrendered to his persuasive personality, you find you're trapped in the proverbial gilded cage.''

A band of fear tightened around Sunny's chest, and she desperately wanted to call her sons back to her side.

DEAN SHOULDERED HIMSELF out of the pool. He could tell something his mother had said had upset Sunny. As much as he loved his mother, being tactful wasn't one of her strong suits. She was far better at bulldozing her way through organizing a charitable event. She thrived on that kind of challenge.

Sunny was far too vulnerable and innocent to handle a woman who was used to dealing from a position of power. It wasn't a skill anyone who lived in the placid mountain environment of Angeles Crest Highway was likely to learn.

''We Weylins have a rule.'' He gave Sunny an encouraging smile as she looked up at him with troubled eyes. ''Everybody who comes here has to have a good time. And all beautiful, sexy women are thrown into the pool. It's a long-standing Weylin tradition.'' Bending, he slipped one arm under her legs and scooped her up.

''No!'' she cried. The plastic ice-tea glass she'd been holding fell to the concrete patio, spilling its contents.

''Why not? You've got a bathing suit on.'' A modest one by most standards, but seductively attractive to him. ''Besides,'' he whispered, ''you looked like you could use saving from my mother.''

"Yes . . . No." She wrapped her arms around his neck. "You're not playing fair."

"Neither were you when you let me ride on that roller coaster. It's getting-even time."

He stood poised on the edge of the pool. Damn, she felt good—slender and supple—and he wondered how he could ever have forgotten, amnesia or not. No curve or soft, tender bit of flesh had slipped his mind since they had last made love. Had it been a week? An eternity seemed closer to the truth.

"Take a deep breath," he ordered.

"Dean, no." She buried her head against his shoulder, and he knew that's where he always wanted her to be. But he wasn't at all confident he could make that happen. Or if he deserved it. In spite of his recent steps toward recovery, he was still basically unemployed. And until he finished his residency, he had little to offer a woman.

He took a step forward. They plunged into the deep end of the pool together.

Air bubbles spiraled up around them in a cloud of foam. Their legs tangled. Her body was slick and achingly familiar against his—the curve of her hip, her slender waist, breasts that pressed to his chest in a way that he knew instinctively belonged crushed against him. Dean fought his instantaneous arousal. Thank goodness the boys had gone off with his father, and the sunlight refracting through the water distorted and disguised his reaction from anyone who might glance in his direction.

He didn't want to embarrass Sunny or himself. Between them, they had far too many issues to work out. He wasn't about to guess at the long-term outcome. At the moment, he simply knew he wanted her beyond all reason.

Sunny gasped as they reached the surface. "Are you trying to drown me?"

"Not likely." A pulse beat at her throat, right where he wanted to kiss her. "I can think of a lot of other things I'd rather do with you."

Trying to catch her breath, she clung to his shoulders. The muscular expanse of his chest tempted her to touch him there, where his nipples puckered from the cold. A fine furring of matted hair arrowed downward, inviting her further exploration.

His knee slid between her legs. At first she thought the movement had been accidental. Then, with his hands at her bare midriff, he shifted her closer until she was riding him, feeling his hair-roughened thigh brushing against the sensitive skin of her inner leg, the press of him in her most intimate place, and she knew it had been intentional. She floated in a warm, sensual sea of wanting.

Gritting her teeth against the delicious sensations, she stifled a groan. "Dean—"

"I know. My timing is lousy."

"Hey, Mom," Danny called from the open French doors to the recreation room. "You want me to throw you the life preserver?"

"No, dear, that won't be necessary." To escape the emotions that had snared her, she'd need far more than a standard-issue, pool-size life preserver.

With infinite slowness, Dean released her. She floated free and treaded water, reluctant to finally sever the connection between them.

Then she turned and stroked alone toward the shallow end of the pool.

HARRINGTON splashed Chivis Regal onto the ice cubes in a glass, then set the crystal decanter back on the polished mahogany bar. "You want another beer?" he asked Dean.

Lifting his bottle to show it was still half-full, Dean said, "I'm fine, thanks." After changing clothes, he'd come back downstairs and found his father in the billiard room waiting for the women to reappear and dinner to be served. The twins were ensconced in the TV room, the walls covered with family photos and shelves decorated with assorted trophies earned years ago by Dean and Rick, who was due to show up any minute. The boys were thrilled with the big screen that made a football stadium appear almost full-size.

"I've talked to Alex Sloan," Harrington said. "He's ready to have you come back on the surgery staff next week."

"I think it's a little premature, sir."

"You said your recovery was going well."

"It is, but I still have a lot of blank spots in my memory." A good many of the most troubling ones related to Sunny and why he'd walked away from her.

"I'd planned to spend the next couple of weeks reviewing surgical procedures and reading the current literature. I'd hate to make any mistakes with a scalpel in my hand."

"Sloan will cover for you, son. It's time you were back where you belong."

"I'll think about it, sir."

Harrington obviously didn't like his answer, but he let it slide, though Dean knew his father had retreated only temporarily. He could be a very tenacious man once his mind was made up.

"You were right about Howie," Harrington said, sipping thoughtfully on his scotch. "He's a bright youngster."

"Yes, sir. Both the boys are."

"I've been thinking you might like to invite Howie down to the hospital. We could give him a tour of the place. Nothing like getting a little firsthand knowledge when you're young."

Putting out the welcome mat was a pleasant change from his father's initial reaction to hearing about the boys. "Howie would probably like that and so would Danny."

Harrington frowned. "I understood from you that Danny wasn't performing well in school. It hardly seems right to build up his hopes for a career in medicine when there is little likelihood—"

"Dad, Danny isn't retarded. He'll be able to chose any career he wants. He'll just have to work a little harder than other people. And what makes you think

Howie will be interested in medicine? Have you asked him?''

''He said something about being an astronaut,'' Harrington groused. ''But that's nonsense. The Weylins have medicine in their veins.''

''I didn't, Dad.'' Rick strolled into the room in an easy, unhurried stride. In a typical act of rebellion, he hadn't dressed up to visit his family. His jeans looked old, his running shoes even more decrepit. ''The sight of blood still makes me sick to my stomach.''

Harrington's frown turned into a scowl. ''You would have gotten over that if you'd given yourself half a chance.''

''I didn't want to.'' Grinning, he extended his hand to Dean. ''I hear congratulations are in order, big bro. How does it feel to be a father?''

''Pretty darn good.''

''Let me take a wild guess. Is the mother that classy lady you brought by my shop a couple of weeks back.''

''The same.''

''Good choice.'' Rick walked behind the bar, retrieved a beer from the small refrigerator and twisted it open. ''So when are you going to make an honest woman of her?''

''What?''

''Now wait a minute, son. Dean's in no position to—''

''She's had his kids, Dad. Seems to me he ought to be thinking about—''

''It's not that easy,'' Dean said.

"Yeah? Does that mean the lady is available? Because if she is, I'm gonna make a play for her, big bro. Just give me the green light." Rick grinned at him, a Weylin smile filled with smug, masculine determination. His blue eyes sparked with devilment.

The ugly fingers of jealousy twisted through Dean's gut like white-hot pokers. His brother had women at his feet and a multimillion dollar business in his back pocket. In contrast, in spite of the progress he'd made, Dean wasn't sure if he'd ever be employable again as anything more than a roadhouse waiter. And he wouldn't know until he reentered the residency program. After all she'd been through, Sunny deserved the very best. So did his sons.

"Keep your distance, Rick," he advised tautly, renewing his vow to prove himself in the arena he knew best—medicine.

"I will." He lifted his beer in salute. "For now."

"HEY, DEAN, that was great!" Howie tumbled into the back seat of the car for the trip home. "You see me go off the diving board? Man, I wish we had a pool."

"Me, too," Danny echoed. He snapped his seat belt in place.

"And that big-screen TV. Wow! Can we get one of those, Mom?"

"No, Howie, the set we have is just fine." She closed the door behind her son. Nineteen inches was plenty big enough to handle reruns of "Gilligan's Island." The boys watched far too much television as it was and would be much better off if they spent more time at their studies.

Dean tossed a smile over his shoulder as he got into the passenger seat of Sunny's car. "You guys can come visit anytime you want. Think of it as your, ah, second home."

"Yeah, neat."

"Can we bring Billy sometime?"

"Sure. Your friends will always be welcome."

Danny nudged Howie in the ribs with his elbow.

As Sunny turned the ignition key and switched on the lights, she heard the boys whispering and giggling. She didn't have the energy to deal with whatever Mischief and Trouble were up to right now. "Settle down, boys," she told them. It was well after dark. After the twins' bedtime, too. And long past the time when her patience had run out with the senior Dr. Weylin's superior attitude.

Anxious to get home, she wheeled the car out of the driveway. "Your brother is a lot of fun," she commented to Dean. Rick had been her salvation during dinner, making jokes when the conversation lagged, which had been all too frequent.

"That's probably why he's known as such a ladies' man," Dean grumbled.

She shot a glance in Dean's direction. If she hadn't known better, she would have thought his terse comment was due to jealousy.

She smiled to herself. If she'd thought for a minute that was true, she would have been happy to flirt back with Rick. Not that she would have meant it. Rick was cute in a boyishly handsome way. Her heart, however, had always belonged to Dean.

Chapter Twelve

Sunny couldn't find Pop.

Still unnerved by the afternoon and evening spent with Dean's family, she'd put her sleepy twins to bed after a mostly quiet ride home. Dean had appeared engrossed in his own thoughts as she had driven the winding road up the hill. She hadn't wanted to interrupt, mentally tangling instead with her own fears and insecurities.

Only after the boys had been safely tucked in had she realized Pop wasn't in his bedroom. Nor were there any lights on downstairs. The roadhouse was closed and locked for the night.

Apprehension skittered along her spine. Had he had another heart attack? Had the stress of running the roadhouse, even with a couple of helpers, been too much for him?

She never should have left him on his own. There was no way she belonged in a fancy Beverly Hills house, not even as a reluctant visitor. She should have stayed right here, looking after her grandfather and the business.

Half expecting to find him collapsed on the kitchen floor, she hurried downstairs and checked there first. The room was dark and empty.

So was the dining room.

Her anxiety increased as she headed into the bar. In the window behind the cash register, the neon Closed sign glowed red. Silence added to her growing panic.

She swallowed thickly. "Pop!"

"I'm right here, missy. No need to get yourself all in a tizzy."

Whirling, she found him sitting at the corner table. She breathed a sigh of relief. "My gosh, I've been looking everywhere for you. Are you all right?"

"Fit as an old man be, I reckon."

"What on earth are you doing sitting in the dark? When I couldn't find you—"

"Been thinking on the future, missy. Yours and them sweet little boys of yours."

Troubled by the despair in his voice, she slid into the chair opposite him. "Are you sure you're okay? No chest pains?"

"Not a one." He took her hands between his age-roughened palms. "This here roadhouse is a heavy yoke I've been wearing for a lot of years, Sunny. Been thinking maybe it's time for me to sell out."

Shock and surprise slammed into her. This wasn't like her grandfather at all. He'd always sworn he'd never leave his beloved mountains. "If you're worried about the finances again, we'll manage. I know we will.''

"We won't unless the snows come early this year. That's about as likely to happen as a hard freeze in August. Figure if we sell, we might walk away with a little change in our pockets. Not much, but enough to see us through for a while.''

"But, Pop, this has been your life for more than fifty years. I was born here and so were the boys. Where would we go?''

His thumb rasped over her knuckles. "Got me a letter from Luke Pardine yesterday. You remember him, don't you?''

"Of course. Your checkers buddy.'' Pop had mourned his friend's decision to move to Arizona several years back and had never since found someone with whom he could share his passion for the game.

"He's bought himself a fancy mobile home in one of them old folks' places. Says it's real nice. They got checkers matches most every day at lunchtime.''

"Pop, you've always said you don't like the desert. It's too hot for you.''

"Can't be all that bad if Luke likes it. Most everywhere has air-conditioning, he says.'' He lifted his shoulders in a discouraged shrug. "It'd be nice to play checkers again.''

"What about me and the boys, Pop? We're hardly ready for a retirement home. And Arizona is a long way away.'' Hundreds of miles from Dean, the father of her twins. The man she loved.

"I've been holding you back, Sunny. I realize that now." He squeezed her hands. "I shouldn't have draped that same heavy yoke around your neck that I've been carrying. You're still young. You need to get on with your life without having to worrying about an old codger like me."

"Pop, you're important to me...to us...we're a family. I can't simply stop worrying—"

"We'd keep in touch. You and the boys, you could come visit during vacations and such."

"Why are you doing this?" She'd been teetering on the edge of an emotional precipice ever since Dean showed up at the roadhouse. Every day it became harder and harder to keep her equilibrium, and today had been the worst, facing Dean's parents and hearing the veiled threat that his father might want to take the twins from her. She couldn't handle her own grandfather essentially throwing her out of the only home she'd ever known. Not now.

Hysteria threatened her control.

She stood abruptly. "You're talking nonsense, Pop. You know you don't want to leave the mountains. You'd hate it in Arizona. This is our home!"

Pop sat very still as Sunny ran from the room. It weren't like he really wanted to go anywhere. But he figured if he didn't cut down her choices and give her a good nudge, Sunny would plant her stubborn streak right smack in front of what she oughta be doing—marrying up with that good-lookin' fella she fell for years ago. If it meant Pop had to bow out of the picture so she could see things straight, so be it.

He scrubbed his fist across his eyes. Wasn't likely playing checkers with that ol' reprobate Luke would be a whole lot of fun anymore, not if he was so far from his home.

DEAN HEARD the screen door slam. Staring up into the darkness surrounding him in his van, he waited for some other sound to tell him who'd come outside and why.

Like a sloughing breeze brushing through the highest branches of a pine tree, her sobs came to him softly.

He eased himself out of bed. Not that he'd been anywhere near asleep. That visit with his parents would have given anyone insomnia. He suspected it had had the same effect on Sunny. Tugging on his jeans, he slid open the door as quietly as possible. Walking gingerly, since he hadn't bothered to put on shoes, he went to her. The full moon cast a brilliant white glow across the clearing.

"Come here." He pulled her to him.

She resisted. "No. I can't do this. Not now."

"Shh. I'm just going to hold you. That's all." He wanted far more than that. But he wanted to comfort her, too, no matter what was troubling her. Truth was, he suspected he was at the crux of her problem.

"You don't understand. Everything's been falling apart since you came back. Now Pop wants to sell the roadhouse, and I have no idea how I'm going to support the boys. Your parents hate me and you're going to take the twins away from me." She pounded her fists on his chest. "It's not fair, dammit! All I ever did wrong was fall in love."

Secretly pleased by her final comment, he pulled her closer so she couldn't beat on him anymore. He'd never seen her so upset. It was hard to know which of her wildly erratic statements he should respond to first. Or if he ought to simply take her into his van and make love to her until she calmed down enough to talk reasonably. Which is what he wanted to do. Though he wasn't so sure she'd be all that thrilled with his antidote for emotional distress.

So he picked the one comment he knew didn't make sense. "Why would you believe I'm going to take the boys away from you?"

"Because you said...then your mother told me..." Her voice caught. "Your father is determined to have a long line of Weylins who are doctors."

It was easy to fill in the missing blanks and each one of them enraged Dean a little more. "My father doesn't have anything to say about what happens to Danny and Howie." He didn't deserve to, after the way he'd dismissed Danny in favor of his more academically gifted twin. He'd done the same damn thing with Dean's brother, Rick. "I told you we'd work things out between us. I still mean that."

"If Pop sells..." She gulped a shaky breath. "I'm going to have to find another job."

Or another man, Dean thought grimly. One who could support her in the way she deserved. And love her, too. Jealousy rocketed through him again. His brother would be right at the front of the line.

"Don't make any rash decisions," he urged. In a desperate need to bind Sunny to him, Dean kissed the top of her head, then her forehead, and searched for her lips. Her breath fluttered in a sigh of surrender. It was the only invitation he needed.

He claimed her mouth with his, hard and fast. His tongue penetrated, searching for all that he wanted, all that he had lost.

In a flash of memory, the image of a rock-lined grotto came to him—a sandy beach where the winter creek widened and turned, a pine tree that had been bent as a sapling into a caricature of a humped-back old man. Dean saw it as clearly as if he were there—Sunny lying on a blanket, her sculpted body naked and beautiful in the noonday sun. And he was with her, loving her.

Breathless with the power of the image, he broke the kiss. "You're coming with me, Sunny. I remember..."

"Remember what?"

"You'll see."

He left her standing there, shaken by his kiss, wondering what he was talking about, as he ducked back into the van. He reappeared an instant later, hopping on one foot as he pulled on the second shoe. A blanket was tucked under his arm.

"It's got to be the full moon," she complained, exasperated that she had reacted so quickly to Dean's kiss. "You and Pop are both acting crazy." And so was she. Her emotions had been vacillating wildly all day, one minute so upset she couldn't manage a coherent thought, and the next so eager to have Dean make love to her, she knew she must surely be going mad.

"I need to know that what I just remembered is real, not some figment of my imagination." He caught her hand. "It's this way, isn't it? There's a path behind the toolshed."

"A path to where?"

"To the clearing where we used to make love."

"It's the middle of the night. We can't—" But they could, she realized. The path would be easy to follow in the moonlight. After the terrible stress of the day, she needed to release the tension that had been building inside her. Her heart ached for things that had been taken from her and those she could possibly lose. Dean. The only home she'd ever known. A grandfather who was aging before her eyes. And her sons, whom she vowed never to give up.

But mostly, she ached for Dean to ease the velvet cord of desire that knotted her reason.

Pulling her along, Dean ducked under a low branch by the toolshed. She followed. She'd claim a few hours of his love as her right, even if it was only an illusion. Then when she grew as old as Pop, she'd have this memory to savor.

Her spirits spiraled upward as they traveled the familiar path. It was like going back in time, to her youth, when love was fresh and good. Her breathing accelerated. She laughed aloud. "We're both crazy!"

"Feels good, doesn't it?" He grinned over his shoulder at her.

"Yes."

An owl took flight on the whisper of wings, startling Sunny as his shadow passed across the moon. She cried out.

"Don't worry. According to local Indian legend, that's a good omen."

"How do you know that?"

"I don't. I just made it up."

She sputtered another laugh and failed to watch where she was stepping. She stumbled over a rock.

Turning, Dean scooped her up into his arms before she could fall. "See, what did I tell you? That wise old owl is helping me out."

"Dean, you can't carry—"

"Hush, woman. I'm being manly. Besides, this is an important research mission. Has Dr. Weylin's memory actually been restored, or is he simply set on seducing the prettiest woman around?"

"The *only* woman."

"The principle is the same."

She snuggled into his embrace. She wasn't sure what had brought on Dean's lighthearted mood, but she loved it. She remembered how his wry humor had made her laugh before. Until now, she'd been afraid that special attribute had fallen victim to his gunshot wound along with the recollection of their past together. But now both memories seemed to be reappearing.

His breathing was labored when they arrived at the sandy bend in the creek. Slowly he lowered Sunny to her feet. He framed her face with his hands.

"Danny and Howie should have been looking here for gold," he said, his voice raspy from exertion. "Your hair is the color of every precious metal I can think of. In the moonlight it shines like golden filaments streaked with silver. Rich. Worth a fortune." His long fingers tunneled through her hair and she couldn't recall ever feeling so thoroughly feminine, so desirable. "I can't remember. Did we ever come here at night like this?"

Her answer whispered across the silent clearing. "Never."

"Good. Then this will be like our first time. A brand-new experience for us both."

He was right. With slow hands, he explored her face in intimate detail, learning each feature with exquisite gentleness before moving on to the sensitive column of her neck. When his fingers delved lower, investigating the buttons on her blouse, releasing them, and finally finding the hook of her bra, she sighed at the sheer, decadent pleasure of his leisurely touch. He cupped her breasts as he exposed them to the rays of the moon. Her knees grew weak.

"You have very talented hands," she said.

"A surgeon needs a light touch."

"Experienced, too."

"Possibly. But having a natural talent is the secret of success."

He dipped his head to suckle her breast. Her breath caught as delicious sensations tingled through her entire body. "I believe I detect a certain amount of arrogance on your part, Dr. Weylin."

"No more than is appropriate," he agreed, teasing her other breast with his tongue.

She tangled her fingers through his wild, cowlick-filled hair. "I think maybe we ought to lie down before—" He nibbled her gently and she lost her train of thought in a choked cry of pleasure.

Somehow Dean managed to extricate himself long enough to spread the blanket on the ground. He yanked off his shirt and tossed it aside. The passion he'd been forced to leash for days was close to exploding.

He gazed at Sunny across the expanse of the blanket. With her blouse hanging open, her breasts were caught by the moonlight, her nipples puckering in the cool night air were dark against her fair complexion. The long, silken strands of her hair hung over one shoulder in a tantalizing drape that hid nothing. She was the most powerfully sexy woman he had ever seen, or ever imagined.

"Sunny, I need to know that you want this as much as I do."

In the stillness of the night, her gaze flicked over him, taking in the expanse of his chest and lowering to discover the strain of his jeans across his pelvis. She met his eyes, then carefully undid the belt of her slacks and lowered her zipper. She stripped slowly, keeping him breathless with anticipation.

When she finished, she knelt on the blanket and extended her hand. "Dean."

He gave a hoarse cry. "Yes, oh Lord, yes."

His own jeans discarded in a heap, he joined her on the blanket and pulled her into his arms. Shivery trembles shuddered through her body. He caressed sweet velvet, warm silk. Each new discovery was like finding something long lost and yearned for even when there'd been no name to assign to what had been missing.

She moved sinuously against him, crying his name softly, urging him closer with fierce determination.

Sunny gasped when he left her embrace. The moon caught the silver glint of a packet he removed from his jeans pocket.

Returning to her, he whispered, "I thought for a while I'd wasted my emergency trip to the drugstore a couple weeks ago."

"No, it wasn't a waste."

He settled between her legs and she lifted her hips in joyous welcome, even as a touch of sadness spread through her awareness. A wise man—or woman—took precautions to avoid an unexpected, unwanted pregnancy.

But the thought was fleeting as he entered her with a fierce thrust. She instantly spun out of control in the madness of moonlight and magic, good omens spinning their fiery filaments of gold around her in a web of desire. Unsure if any of this was real, she touched his face, the whiskers on his jaw, and dug her fingernails into his sleek, sweat-dampened shoulders. She pressed her mouth to his, finding his taste minty fresh.

For years she had dreamed this would be true—her lost Dean returned. Even as she reached her peak and plummeted over the top, in some tiny, frightened spot within her, she was still afraid to believe it was so.

DEAN'S RESPIRATION slowly returned to normal. When he rolled away, he pulled Sunny with him, holding her so he cushioned her from the rocky ground. He kept on touching her, learning and re-learning the swell of her breast, the velvety crook of her elbow, the silken feel of her hair feathering his chest. The shape of her belly and how it fit against his took on new meaning as he recalled that she had carried his babies there.

He was a father.

He had obligations to both Sunny and the twins, responsibilities he'd either ignored or avoided for too long. Somehow, he had to make up for that and find a way to make them all proud of him.

"My father wants me to come back to the hospital and start working as soon as I can. That means I'll have to move back home."

She went very still in his arms. "The twins will miss you."

"I'll get back up here as often as I can." He left unsaid that long shifts and backbreaking studies would keep him away more than he'd like. There was no point in dwelling on the negatives. "I'll be through with my residency in May. In the meantime, we'll all have a chance to get reacquainted. I'd like the boys to know—"

"Of course. I understand."

Her body going rigid, and her voice taut, she withdrew from him both physically and mentally, as if she wanted to sever any connection between them. The cool air brushed across his chest, raising gooseflesh along with a sense of dread.

"We'd better get back," she said. "It's late."

He didn't want the evening to end, not this way. "You know I can't make any serious plans until I get my own life together. It's hard to even think about the future."

"Don't worry about it, Dean." Turning her back, she put on her blouse. "I understand about your priorities. I'm sure you'll be a very fine doctor."

THE BAG OF FLOUR slipped from her hands and spilled across the counter.

Sunny swore. Loudly.

It was the third thing she'd dropped that morning. Of course, lack of sleep the previous evening was no doubt the reason. She'd been a fool last night. Once again she would have to make a future for herself that didn't include Dean. This time, Pop might not even be there to provide the stability both she and the twins needed.

At the moment, she didn't know who to vent her fury on—Dean, Pop, or more appropriately, herself.

Still, she hadn't been this inept in the kitchen since she'd been pregnant with the twins. The obstetrician had assured her that hormonal imbalance could cause all sorts of side effects, including being a klutz.

Thirsty, she went to the refrigerator and pulled out a bottle of grapefruit juice. She held it carefully as she poured a glass. No way did she want to have a sticky mess to clean up on the kitchen floor.

She took a big swig, enjoying the cold tartness as it slipped down her throat.

It hit the bottom of her empty stomach and bounced.

"Oh, my God—" She dashed for the sink. Grapefruit juice never affected her this way...

Her thoughts slowed to an absolute crawl and she tried to reject the implication of what was going through her mind. The first time they'd made love, Dean hadn't used any protection. Her hormones had been on a rampage for the past week or so. Now that she thought about it, her normally regular period was late, the first time...

...since she had been pregnant with the twins.

"No-o-o," she groaned and was promptly and desperately ill.

Chapter Thirteen

"I'm as fertile as a damn rabbit!"

Mindy hugged her. "You can't know that for sure, hon. You haven't actually taken a test, have you? Maybe you're just late—"

"All Dean has to do is look at me sideways and boom! I'm pregnant."

"Funny, Quinn and I used a different technique. Maybe we ought to try—"

"This is no laughing matter, Mindy."

"I'm sorry, hon, but I don't see the problem. The timing may be off, but you love the guy, don't you?"

"I loved him nine years ago. What's that got to do with anything?"

"Well, I thought..." Mindy's perfectly arched eyebrows lowered. "He doesn't love you?"

"He's certainly never said so. And besides, he's got that damn surgical residency to finish. He's already told me he won't have much time to play daddy to the twins until next May. Can you imagine what he'll say if I announce I'm about to add one more tiny bundle of joy to his life? He'll walk away so fast—''

''Are you really that sure?''

Sunny took a deep, shaky breath and stared out the window. Mindy's home was little more than a cottage provided by the Forest Service. Outside, a green utility four-wheel-drive vehicle was parked by a service building, and there was a huge pile of split wood ready for the coming winter. Inside, the decor included cheerful calico slipcovers and flounces that accented the pine furniture. It was warm and inviting, the first place Sunny had thought to go when she realized the desperate mistake she'd made—again.

''He wants to be a doctor, Mindy. His father wants him to be a doctor. Even his mother wants him to be a doctor. Dean once told me he'd made up his mind by the time he was ten that he was going to be a doctor.'' The words came out in a singsong of despair. She wrapped her arms around her midsection to stop herself from trembling so hard. ''He never once told me he *wanted* to be a father, not until he discovered the boys were his. My getting pregnant with them was an accident. And now it's happened a second time. You must think I'm the world's worst fool.''

''No, I think you're a woman in love. That excuses a lot of stuff.''

''Stupidity included.''

''More often than we would care to admit, I imagine.'' Mindy poured a cup of coffee from the pot and gestured to a chair at the lacquered pine kitchen table. "Sit down, hon. Things are never as bad as they seem." She placed the mug in front of Sunny.

"They're worse," Sunny wailed, insecurities and fears gurgling up in an unpleasant mix of emotional stew. "I can't even have caffeine. Last time I spent the whole nine months asleep on my feet." She drew a gulping breath. "Oh, Mindy, what am I going to do?"

Bringing her own mug of coffee to the table, Mindy sat down opposite Sunny. "How did he react when he learned the twins were his?"

"At first he was furious with me—that I'd kept them a secret. Then he was..." Men weren't normally ecstatic. Euphoric didn't seem like the right description, either. "He thought he was the first man since Adam to have fathered a baby, much less two of them."

Mindy grinned. "The guy's absolutely normal. Quinn was the same way. He strutted around for the full nine months and then nearly passed out in the delivery room."

"That doesn't mean Dean wants to be a father of another child. It certainly couldn't be a part of his plan. He still has his residency..." Nor did his enthusiasm for the twins suggest for a minute that Dean loved her, Sunny thought dejectedly. And *that,* she realized in some painful spot near her heart, was the real problem.

"His medical training is *his* problem, Sunny. Not yours. This will be put-up or shut-up time. It's that simple."

Sunny didn't think any of this was simple. The pregnancy made things impossibly complicated. Pop wanted to move away. She'd likely be leaving, too. Her children—all three of them—would, for all practical purposes, have no father. Or at least they wouldn't have a father who had eagerly sought that role. She hadn't forced him to accept that role nine years ago— or to marry her out of obligation—and didn't want to do so now.

Covering Sunny's hands where she'd wrapped them tightly around the warm mug, Mindy said, "Just tell him, hon. Put the ball in his court. There's no man on this planet you can outguess. They're all from Mars."

In spite of herself, Sunny's lips twitched. So far she'd made a dismal mess of her relationship with Dean, as if they had indeed come from two different planets. But she wouldn't make the same mistake twice. This time she'd tell him the truth. And then, no matter what the outcome, get on with her life.

"So," Mindy said, seeing Sunny's smile, "how do you feel about the kid?"

Instinctively Sunny's hand flew to her abdomen. She'd been so wrapped up in the shock of being pregnant, that she hadn't given much thought to the baby. There'd been no time to relish the knowledge that a new life was growing inside her. *Dean's child.* A daughter, maybe, with golden hair and blue eyes, and a streak of her mother's stubbornness. Or another boy with a mischievous grin. How could she not love this child as much as she had those she'd already borne?

"I think I've been more than twice blessed," she said with conviction. She could only hope Dean might feel the same way.

LAUGHTER GREETED Sunny when she arrived at the back door of the roadhouse. There'd been a precipitous drop in the temperature since she'd left that morning, and the feel of snow was in the air. Shivering, she recalled how every winter she'd battled with the boys to keep the warmth in the roadhouse and not let it escape into the outside. This season appeared to be off to a similar start.

Amid all of her careening emotions and the errands she'd had to run after commiserating with Mindy, she'd forgotten it was a short school day. The boys were already home. So was Dean. And none of them had thought to close the door.

To her surprise, she saw through the screen that Stevie, the adolescent sniper, had joined the trio at the kitchen table. He looked even dirtier and more haggard than the night they'd discovered him at the fire lookout, except now there was a mustache of milk on his upper lip, and an empty glass and plate in front of him.

Danny spotted her first. "Hey, Mom, come see what we're doing. Dean thought up a neat game."

The hinges protested as she opened the door. For weeks she'd been meaning to oil them. Now it didn't seem important at all.

Dean turned and his gaze met hers. What would he say when she broke the news of her pregnancy to him? Somehow she doubted he'd be all that pleased.

"Go ahead, Howie," Danny urged. "Show Mom."

Howie shuffled through a stack of five-by-seven cards, finally selected one with the word Laugh printed on it and showed it to the assembled group. Danny immediately burst into raucous laughter.

"You missed that one, Dean," Howie chortled. "Danny beat you."

"I was watching your mother. She's lots prettier than you are."

"Oh, yuck. Dean's getting mushy over Mom," Danny complained.

"Try this one." Undaunted by inattentive students, Howie flashed another card.

After a moment's hesitation, Danny leaped to his feet and began jumping around the kitchen in response to the word Jump printed on the card.

Sunny's heart swelled with love and pride, as well as more than a smidgen of optimism. With enough help, she believed her son would be able to succeed at whatever he chose to do with his life. "That's very good, honey." Smiling, she caught her pogo-stick son and gave him a quick kiss, then slid her attention to their visitor. "Hello, Stevie."

Without looking up, he mumbled, "'Lo."

She sent a questioning look in Dean's direction.

"Stevie was getting kind of tired of hanging around on his own up here in the mountains," Dean explained, his expression restrained. "And the nights are getting pretty cold. I figured he could use a little something to eat, so I fixed him a sandwich.''

"Dean called Stevie's mom.'' Howie shifted the cards in his hands. ''She says he can come home if he wants.''

"Oh?'' What about calling the police? Sunny wondered. The sheriff would probably be interested to know the sniper had turned himself in.

As if reading her mind, Dean said, ''I thought if Stevie could go home, he'd be better off than if he was sent to juvenile hall. Except for scaring a few people, he hasn't done all that much damage.''

Sunny eyed the boy. Sympathetically, she asked, "Did your mother have a change of heart?''

"Mom said she's been worried about me. And the guy she'd been shackin' up with has cut out. Without him . . .'' Stevie gave a halfhearted shrug. ''It won't be so bad. He was always on my case. Mom didn't wanna make waves.''

"I talked to Stevie's mother about getting him into a special school,'' Dean said. ''She seemed to think that was a good idea. I'm going to ask Rick to give her some advice.''

Hardly able to take on the burden of another child, Sunny simply nodded her agreement. She wanted Stevie to be all right. Maybe, under different circumstances, she'd have taken more interest in his troubles. But the truth of the matter was, at this particular moment, she had plenty of her own problems to face.

She glanced around the kitchen. The thought of cooking, and all the smells that went with it, made her stomach threaten rebellion. The first three months of her pregnancy with the boys had been the pits. It felt as if this time around wouldn't be much of an improvement.

She sighed. Carelessness was a harsh teacher.

"Stevie's mother is picking him up," Dean said. "She ought to be here in a half hour or so."

"Fine. I'll just go upstairs..." And try not to be sick.

BY THE TIME she'd splashed cold water on her face, made an effort to compose herself and come back downstairs to start dinner preparations, Stevie was gone. Only Dean remained in her kitchen.

"Look, I'm going to have to go back to work by the end of this week," Dean said. His golden-brown eyebrows were leveled in concern; tension tightened his sensual lips. "Dad insists. And frankly, I'm anxious to get through my residency as soon as I can. I thought... Well, there's an hour or two before we're likely to get any kind of a dinner rush. I thought this would be a good time to call the boys in and tell them I'm their father. Then they'd have a couple of days to get used to the idea before I have to leave."

Leave. The word created a tangle of fear and anxiety that knotted in Sunny's uneasy stomach. In spite of the twins—and now this new pregnancy—she had no right to hold him if he didn't want to stay. "There's another detail you need to know before you tell them about...us."

"What's that?"

She swallowed hard. "I'm pregnant." *Again.*

In the silence that followed, she heard the clock above the stove ticking. Outside, a jay squawked and a car went by on the road. The muffled voices of the twins drifted down from somewhere upstairs. Dean simply stared at her in mute disbelief.

When he found his voice, it was hoarse and choked. "You're kidding."

"Not likely." Though she'd expected something less than enthusiasm, it still hurt more than she'd thought possible. He didn't want her or the babies she seemed to conceive with such ease.

"We used protection."

"Not the first time."

He swore softly. "Okay." He paced across the room, his fingers plowing through his hair. The shock of Sunny's announcement rattled through his complacency. He was going to have to make a decision and make it fast. This new complication was his fault. The timing was terrible. But he cared about Sunny. A lot. And the boys, too. And there was only one thing he could do. Feeling like a surgeon about to make his first cut, he took a deep breath before laying out the protocol he'd chosen.

"Okay, we'll get married. We can make it to Las Vegas for a day or two, and I can still get back before—"

"No."

His head snapped up. He scowled. "What do you mean, no?" He'd never in his life proposed to a woman and hadn't expected to be turned down when he finally did. Certainly not by a woman who was pregnant with his child—for the second time. "Maybe you didn't understand me. I think we ought to get married as soon as—"

"Why? I didn't force you into marrying me nine years ago when I realized I was pregnant. I don't see any reason to marry you now simply because I've gotten myself into the same fix again." However foolishly.

"Last time you didn't bother to tell me you were going to have my kid...ah, kids, rather. This time I know. I'll do the right thing by you."

Only her pride kept Sunny's chin up in the face of his statement. What she wanted was his love; what he offered was duty.

"Wonderful." Building up a huge case of self-righteous indignation, she spat out the word. "And are you ready to explain to the twins why you're so eager to marry me now, when nine years ago at the mere suggestion that I was pregnant, you did a vanishing act? That will make them feel really good about themselves, won't it?" It certainly didn't make her feel all that good. The truth was a double-edged sword when love wasn't involved.

He blanched. "I can't believe I would have walked out on you, Sunny. Not if I'd actually known you were pregnant. But you've got to remember, I was hardly more than a kid myself."

"An *ambitious* kid, who thought becoming a doctor was the most important thing in his life. He was willing to make any sacrifice for his career. Nothing was going to stand in his way. Nothing!'' Fighting the tears that threatened, she hugged her arms to her midsection. Pain knotted her stomach. ''If you can tell me any of that has changed, anything at all, I'll consider your proposal. Otherwise, I'd say the reason I didn't tell you about the twins was a damn good one. You don't want us, Dean Weylin. Not me, nor the boys, nor the baby that's already growing in my belly.''

''That's not true. It's only that I'm not ready—''

''When will you be ready, Dean? After you finish your residency?''

''The timing would be a hell of a lot better then.''

''Then I guess the twins and I had better wait until you can squeeze us into your schedule. And that goes for the baby, too. We certainly wouldn't want to interfere with your career.''

''Look, what more do you want from me? You drop this bombshell in my lap, I'm trying to adjust as fast as I can and you turn down my proposal like I'm some bum off the street.''

Hysteria threatened to make Sunny say a whole lot of things she didn't want to reveal. Such as how much she loved him. How she didn't ever want him to go away. That she wanted him to love her back and find a spot in his life that could be hers and hers alone. Not because she gave birth to his babies, but because he couldn't bear the thought of living without her. Just as she hated the prospect of losing him for a second time.

The words jammed in her throat. What came out was a whispered plea, the echo of the lie she'd been telling herself for the past nine years. "I want you to go away, Dean. I want you to take your van and go back where you belong. I want you to leave us alone."

"You don't mean that."

"Yes, I do. As far as I'm concerned, you're trespassing." Trampling on her heart certainly qualified as a felony in her book.

He stared at her, his eyes narrowed, a muscle working at his jaw. The distance between them was like two mountain peaks separated by a rugged canyon, each inch covered with jagged rocks and spiky cactus spines. A dangerous situation. There seemed no way to bridge the gap.

Making a visible effort to control his anger, he said, "I think we both need to cool off before we discuss this subject further. But I'll be back, Sunny. You can't keep me away forever. The twins are as much mine as they are yours. And so is this new baby."

She held her breath as he marched out the door. The screen groaned then slammed behind him. A moment later the engine on his van roared, gears complained and tires slid on the loose gravel. Through the window, she could see the first few lonely flakes of snow drifting down from the lowering sky.

Possessively Sunny slid her hand across her flat stomach. Dean was gone. She'd sent him away, and he'd allowed her to do so in spite of the fact that she carried his child. He'd felt no joy in her pregnancy. Whether or not he'd actually known or suspected the truth nine years ago, the results were the same. Nothing had changed. She still had her pride, she supposed, and he was still determined to have his career. That was a small comfort that wouldn't keep either of them warm on cold winter nights.

The twins' rapid-fire footsteps announced their arrival downstairs before they appeared. Sunny turned toward the stove and dinner preparations so they wouldn't see the tears in her eyes.

"Hey, Mom, where'd Dean go?" Danny asked.

"He didn't say anything about going into town," Howie complained. "He was gonna help me put together a model airplane, that real complicated one you got me last Christmas. Pop couldn't even figure out how it went together."

She chewed on her lower lip, searching to explain what she couldn't fully understand herself. "Boys, Dean had to go back to work, to the hospital. He's going to be a big, important doctor—"

"You mean he's left for good?"

"Isn't he coming back?"

"He may come back," she told them carefully. "But for now he has to learn all he can about being a doctor. It's very important to him."

Howie's face scrunched up into a disbelieving frown. "He didn't even say goodbye. Danny and me thought—"

"That was probably my fault." She ran a soothing hand over Howie's head, over his achingly familiar cowlick-ridden curls, so like his father's. "He and I sort of had an argument." A large part of which had been her fault, she admitted, hormones and insecurities combining in a destructive way. But if he'd loved her—truly loved her—he'd have understood. He would have held her and kissed her and told her it was all right. If the man had any sense at all, that's how he would have acted.

Wrapping his arms around Sunny's midsection in a loving hug, Danny said, ''It's okay, Mom. He likes us a whole lot. Us guys whose brains are all scrambled sometimes have to run away, but we come back. You'll see.''

Her chin trembled and she hugged him back. Sunny hoped her son was right. But she didn't dare count on it.

THE TWINS were upstairs taking their baths when Pop came into the kitchen.

''The last of the customers just left, tryin' to get themselfs down the hill before the snow builds up too much. Looks like we're in for a full-fledged blow. TV says the storm may last more'n a day or two.''

''Yes. And that means Gene will be able to open his ski area before Thanksgiving.'' She scraped the remaining beans into a plastic container. ''In fact, we'll probably be busy this weekend. The first snow always drives a lot of people up the mountains to gawk.''

''Sure wish Dean hadn't gone on back to his doctoring school. He oughta be here to help out. It ain't right—''

"Of course it is, Pop. He has his own life to lead. And so do we." Dashing some detergent into the pot, she ran the hot water. Her whole body felt stiff with the effort to control her emotions. "With an early winter like this, I think we might get a good price for the roadhouse. We'll have to talk to a realtor right away, or maybe put an ad in the paper ourselves. We need to strike while the iron's hot, or in this case, cold."

"Missy, what the devil are you talkin' about?"

"You said you wanted to sell the place. And if you're going to Arizona, I don't see any particular reason to stay here. I'm sure I could find employment near where you'll be living. I've certainly had enough experience managing a restaur—"

"Have you gone plum loco? Them twins need a father—"

"I quite agree. In fact, I think I may try to find a job where I'll have some time off. I haven't dated anyone in a long time—"

Pop slammed his palm on the table. "That dadburn fool hasn't just gone back to his schooling! He walked out on you again, didn't he? Why, I ought to get on my horse and go after that no good, sidewinding—" Pop's face turned scarlet. He gasped for breath. "I'll take a whip to him, that's what I'll do."

She eased him into a chair at the table. "No, Pop, please don't be upset with him."

"Didn't you ask him to stay? To take care of you and the boys?"

"He left because it's the right thing for him to do. I told him to go, and he went. It's that simple." And that was painful. But she wasn't going to think about that now. Not yet.

"I can't understand—"

"If he'd stayed, we both would have been unhappy. I'm sure when he has time, he'll develop a relationship with the twins." And the baby, too. "He's an honorable man." So honorable he'd offered marriage when it was the last thing on his mind.

"It's just I hate seeing you alone, missy." He took her hand between his work-roughened palms.

"I'm not alone, Pop. I have you and the boys." And soon she'd have to tell him about the child that was on the way. But not yet. For now she'd hold that knowledge to herself and savor it on her own. Then later...

DAMN! He never should have let Sunny run him off.

Gripping the wheel, Dean tried to concentrated on driving his van, knowing he should have at least taken the time to say goodbye to the boys. That important oversight didn't exactly give him high marks as a dad.

But he'd been stunned by the revelation of Sunny's pregnancy and her refusal to marry him.

"Man, what's a guy supposed to do?" he shouted to no one in particular.

The road down from the mountain had never seemed quite so winding. The slick combination of rain and slush required him to devote all of his attention to driving.

But his mind kept wandering in rhythm to the swipe of the windshield wipers, his thoughts going over the scene he'd just played out with Sunny as if he was a student reviewing a final exam he'd taken—and was sure he had failed. Every word, each facial expression, flashed through his brain. Questions had been asked, answers given.

Still, something didn't compute.

Rubbing his fingertips against his temple, feeling the raised flesh where he'd been wounded, he tried to diagnose the problem. If you didn't ask the right questions, the answers led to the wrong conclusion. In the case of a seriously ill patient, that could be fatal.

Sunny had tossed him out on his ear. The twins not withstanding, she had every right to do that. He'd gotten her pregnant, hadn't he? Twice! Except she hadn't really blown her stitches until he'd proposed.

Frowning, he took a turn a little too fast, and his back wheels slid across the center line. Vans were notoriously hard to manage on this kind of slick surface. Fortunately the storm had kept the traffic down on the mountain road. No oncoming vehicle challenged his right to the whole roadway. He breathed a sigh of relief.

He ought to feel relieved that Sunny hadn't demanded instant marriage. Even in this day and age, most women would have. But she was strong. Sensible. She'd managed on her own, or at least with the help of her grandfather, for a good many years. She didn't need him.

Now, why, he wondered, did that bother him so much?

He had his medical training to finish before he could make any long-term commitment. The fact that he'd felt more at home at the roadhouse with Sunny and the twins than he had at his parents' home was inconsequential. Without a job, a real one, he could hardly expect Sunny to be enamored of the prospect of marriage to him.

His fingers drummed an impatient beat on the steering wheel.

Sunny wasn't the kind of woman who gave herself to just any man, and she didn't give a fig about status. The twins would only be impressed if he could split a cord of wood for the fire in record time. The baby, he assumed, didn't care much one way or the other.

Without knowing quite how he'd arrived there, Dean pulled into the parking lot of University Hospital. Rain glazed the sidewalks and dripped off the covered walkway to the entrance. He brought the van to a halt in one of the physician slots and leaned his head against his arms, which he'd folded across the steering wheel.

Since the age of ten, he had studied to be a doctor. A surgeon. He'd devoted all of his energies toward that goal. Sunny knew that.

When she'd learned she was pregnant with the twins, she'd made every sacrifice necessary to assure he wouldn't fail.

He sat up with a start. "Damn!"

Like a stained-glass window, images of the past flowed together. Sure, there were some seams missing. But he could see what had happened as clearly as if the sun was shining through the pane. He'd failed Sunny once. He didn't intend to let that happen again.

Chapter Fourteen

The van slid and came perilously close to the edge of the cliff before the tires caught and propelled the vehicle a few hundred feet further up the hill. Sweat trickled down between Dean's shoulder blades. He might be on a fool's errand, but he wasn't going to rest until he reached the Cloud High Roadhouse—and Sunny.

With each foot of altitude he gained, he found the snow had stuck more thickly to the road. At the three-thousand-foot marker, there'd been an inch of the white stuff piled on the boulders and weighting the pine branches. Now there was maybe three inches covering everything, and it was coming down harder by the minute.

He shifted into a lower gear. The tires slipped again. This time the van kept on fishtailing in a slow dance that brought the rear bumper into contact with a very large, solid rock. He gunned the engine. The wheels simply dug themselves deeper into the mud and snow at the side of the road.

"Damn!"

With a frustrated twist of his wrist, he switched off the ignition, rummaged in the back of the van to come up with his jacket and picked up what he needed from the passenger seat. As he recalled, Forest Service headquarters was just up the road, and right behind that was the house where Quinn and Mindy lived. Less than a mile from here, he'd guess. Quinn would have a vehicle that could make it the rest of the way to the roadhouse.

Tennis shoes, he rapidly concluded, offered little warmth for walking in six inches of snow. His feet had nearly turned to two chunks of ice by the time he found the turnoff into Quinn's driveway.

Dressed in a flannel robe, Quinn responded to his frantic pounding on the door. "Dean?" he questioned. "Man, do you know what time it is?"

"I need to borrow your four-wheel drive."

That got his attention. "Is it Pop? Did he have another attack?"

"Nope. I'm going up the hill, not down."

Roused by the noise at the door, Mindy peered around her husband. "Dean, you look frozen. Come on in and get warmed up."

"There's no time. I've got to see Sunny."

Her gaze settled on what Dean carried in his hand, and a smile lifted her lips. "Give him the keys, Quinn," she said sweetly.

"The Highway Patrol is about to close the road, hon. I can't let him borrow the Dodge. It's against regulations. Nobody can use the truck except—"

"Just do it, dear. Can't you see you're interfering with a man on a mission?"

"Hey, Mom! What's going on?"

"Nothing, Billy. You go on back to sleep. It's late." She smiled at Dean. "While Quinn's getting the keys, I'll find a warm hat for you and some gloves. I think Sunny would want me to take very good care of you right about now."

He tucked his free hand up under his jacket to warm it with whatever body heat he had. "Thanks, Mindy. I appreciate it."

Returning to the door, Quinn passed over the keys. "Drive careful," he warned, "or it'll be my job."

"You got it." He pulled on the gloves Mindy gave him, started to leave, then turned back. "The road-house is on Forest Service land, isn't it?"

"That's right."

"You suppose the Forest Service would agree to a little remodeling of the place? Maybe an add-on with some nicer living quarters and a small medical office. Nothing fancy. Just enough to handle weekend emergencies, like car and skiing accidents?"

Quinn grinned. "You making some plans, are you?"

"If a certain lady agrees."

"I think I could comfortably recommend that kind of modification in the lease agreement," Quinn said. "Assuming the lady approves, of course."

"I intend to be very persuasive."

SUNNY WAS PROUD of herself.

She hadn't cried all evening. Not a single tear. Instead she'd made much better use of her time by washing the cupboards down and rearranging the stock in the pantry. The floor got a vigorous scrubbing, too, along with a coat of wax. The weekend was likely to be busy. It made sense to be ready.

Finally her arms grew so weary she could hardly lift them, and her legs were about to cave in. Now she'd be able to sleep, she assured herself.

As she went upstairs, the roadhouse felt strangely cold and empty, as though a chill had seeped into the walls since Dean had left. The scent of him haunted her imagination; the warm baritone of his voice echoed in her memory.

She shook her head. These were the same stairs she had traveled every day of her life, the same hallway. There were no voices here except those of her children and grandfather, silent now as they slept. No scents except soap and wax.

The reality of that knowledge struck with such force, she reeled from it. Blindly she stumbled into her room, closed the door and fell onto her bed. Burying her face in her pillow, she wept as she had never wept before.

THE SCREEN CREAKED as he let himself in through the back door, and Dean swore softly under his breath. He didn't want to wake the rest of the family. Reminding Sunny to keep her door locked would wait for another time. In this case, her careless habit worked to his advantage.

By the time he reached the upstairs hallway, he could hear the muffled sobs coming from her room. The sound ripped at him. *His fault,* he realized. He'd been too dense to understand the depth of the sacrifice she had been willing to make—for the second time.

What a pair of fools they were!

He opened the bedroom door and stepped inside, closing it behind him.

The crying stopped on a choked sob.

"Don't stop on my account," he whispered.

"Dean?"

"You had me pretty well fooled when you threw me out. Trespassing? Effectively telling me to get on with my life without you?" She shifted on the bed, making the springs groan, and he sat down beside her. "I got all the way down the hill before I realized you were lying to me."

"I never . . . lie."

"No, that's not true. What you don't do is try to trap a guy. Or put yourself and your needs before what you think he wants."

"Please just go away."

"Not this time." He found her face and palmed it with his hand. She leaned into his touch, as he'd known she would. "See, I was parked in front of the hospital when it all came back to me, or most of it, anyway. Nine years ago you loved me so much you were willing to give me up because you thought that's what I wanted."

"You wanted a career."

"Yeah, but I did love you, Sunny. For months after we stopped seeing each other I just went through the motions. I nearly got myself thrown out of med school. In fact, I suspect that's just what I wanted. But Dad pulled in every favor that was owed him. They didn't toss me."

"You must have been glad."

"Let's just say I carried on because I was too cowardly to do anything else. Certainly I was too much of a chicken to fight my father. I'm sorry, Sunny. God, I'm sorry."

"You don't have to be. I knew..." Her voice caught. "I wanted so much for you to just call. That's all. I wouldn't have forced you—"

"A thousand times I started to call. Once or twice I actually dialed your number. And then I hung up before anyone answered. What did I have to offer you, Sunny? I hardly ever got any time off once school had started again. I didn't have any income of my own, and I knew Dad wouldn't give me a dime if I got married. You deserved better than to be stuck with a starving med student."

"You were making a sacrifice to protect me?"

"That sounds a little more noble than it probably was. Sometimes I used to think that after my residency... but time passed, and eventually I figured you'd probably found someone else."

"I didn't."

"I know." Gratitude constricted his throat as he ran the back of his hand along her tear-dampened cheek. "Then when I got shot and was trying to recuperate, my subconscious sent me back here. To the one place where I felt truly at home. With you.''

She sniffed and sat up, swiping at her hair in a futile effort to make herself more presentable. "Did you know...I mean, didn't you even guess I was pregnant?"

"I swear to you, Sunny, on my word of honor, if I had known what you were trying to tell me, I never would have left you—med school and my father's approval be damned! I was just too dense to realize what you were hinting at." He tucked a bit of straying hair behind her ear. "There's never been any other place, any other time, when I'd felt loved except when I was with you. Loved, not because I was smart, or because I was going to be a doctor or came from a family with money. But simply because of myself."

"You've always been special."

"You're the only one who's ever thought so, Sunny. But you told me no when I proposed earlier. That really confused me. If you'd cried, or begged me to stay—"

"That wouldn't have been fair."

"You're right. I had to figure it out on my own. That way, if anything went wrong I wouldn't be able to blame you for trapping me in a marriage I didn't want."

"I wouldn't do that to you."

"I know. You're too proud and too stubborn for that." He brushed a kiss across her lips. So sweet, so incredibly innocent. "That's why I love you."

She went very still. "You love me?"

"That's what I said." He reached for the light that he knew was next to the bed and fumbled for the switch. They both squinted when the light came on. Sunny's eyes were red-rimmed, her cheeks were splotchy from crying and most of her hair had come loose from her fancy braid. Dean figured he'd never seen her look more beautiful.

He laid a bouquet of flowers across her lap. "I coerced the night janitor at the hospital into opening up the gift shop. I'm afraid these flowers got a little frostbitten." The carnations were drooping and beginning to turn black. The baby's breath didn't look much better.

"They're beautiful. But how did you get here? I didn't hear the snowplow go by and the road has be to closed by now."

"I borrowed Quinn's Dodge Ramcharger. I think he and Mindy approve of me."

"Approve?"

He pulled out the box of chocolates that he had tucked inside his jacket. "I don't know whether these are frozen or melted. But it's the thought that counts."

"Dean, you didn't have to—"

"Sure I did. I really blew my first proposal. I figured I had to start from scratch. You know, flowers and candy."

A little smile tugged at the corners of her lips. "You're going to propose again?"

"I am. I had a little trouble with the ring, though. Hospital gift shops aren't particularly well stocked with diamonds."

"Ring?" She choked on the word as he produced a small ring with tiny violets circling the porcelain.

"I know I'm not all that good a catch," he continued, trying to stave off any argument she might make. "I still need to finish my medical training. The hours will be horrific. But I can certainly wait until the next rotation so we can have some time together. Then I figured I might open a practice in La Canada, right down the hill, and get on staff at Community Hospital, not at University Hospital."

"But you told me the Weylins always became Chief of Staff at University."

"Not me. All I want is to be a doctor and have a family. A home that I can come back to. I talked to Quinn about the Forest Service issuing a permit to expand this place and letting me have an office here for emergencies. You know, on weekends when there are a lot of tourists. It's a long ride for paramedics this far up the hill."

"Could you stop talking for a minute?"

"No, I can't. I need you to know that you're the first and only woman I've ever loved. Or will ever love for the rest of my life. I promise you that. I want you to have my children—dozens of them. And I want us to be a family."

"If you'd take a breath, I'd say yes." She helped him slip the porcelain ring onto her finger.

"You would?"

"Yes, I would." She linked her arms around the back of his neck. "I love you, Dean Weylin. I always have. I can't imagine loving another man. And I'll have as many of your children as you want—within reason. A dozen might be a bit extreme.''

He crushed her to him. ''We're going to have to explain all this to the twins.''

''We will, sweetheart. The morning will be soon enough.'' For now, Sunny simply wanted Dean to herself. Explanations would come later.

SUNNY'S BEDROOM door flew open.

''Mom! It snowed last night. Really hard! Can we make a snowman? Can we—'' Danny came to a quick halt in the middle of the room. ''Dean?'' he asked.

Mortified, Sunny knew her son had correctly identified the warm, masculine body lying next to her in bed. She had the distinct urge to pull the sheet up over her head and disappear. What would the twins think?

''Good morning, son,'' Dean said. Under the covers, his hand stole across her middle. She whacked it away.

Bare feet thudding on the floor, Howie came blasting into the room to join his brother. ''Hey, you're back.''

''I'm back,'' Dean agreed.

''Are you gonna stay this time?''

''You bet I am. In fact, your mother has agreed to marry me.''

''Yeah? Does that mean you're gonna be our dad?''

''Boys,'' Sunny hissed. Her cheeks flamed with embarrassment. ''Could we have this discussion later?'' When both she and Dean were more appropriately dressed for a family meeting.

"It's okay, Mom," Danny said. "Billy's mom and dad sleep together all the time, too. It's what grown-ups do."

She groaned.

"Danny. Howie. What your mother wants you to know is that I'm your real father. I didn't know that until recently because . . . well, she and I had kind of a misunderstanding and she didn't tell me—"

"Oh, heck! We figured that out weeks ago," Howie said.

"How?" Sunny was aghast.

"'Cause you guys were acting so dopey," Danny said. "We figured something weird was going on. Then we saw the picture of Dean and his brother when they were kids. It's there on the wall in the TV room at his house. It's not like we're stupid, you know. Me 'n Howie thought at first it was us, except he wasn't wearing his glasses. Then we figured out what was going on."

Dean's deep chuckle shook the bed. "A couple of wise guys, eh?"

Both boys grinned mischievously.

"So can we make a snowman, Mom?" Danny asked.

"As soon as you get dressed. And put on some warm clothes. Your boots, too."

They both made a dash for the door, but Danny came to an abrupt stop before leaving the room.

"Hey, Dean, you'd better pick your clothes up off the floor before Mom sees 'em. She really hates it when you leave a mess."

"Thanks for the advice, son."

Sputtering, Sunny collapsed into helpless giggles.

Once the boys were out of sight and hearing, Dean leaned over her. "I love you, Sunny McCloud. And I love our sons and the baby we're going to have."

"I love you, too. We all do."

He lowered his head and kissed her, long and deep and lovingly, as he had throughout much of the night and intended to do for the rest of his life.

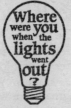

HARLEQUIN®
AMERICAN ◆ ROMANCE®

The Magic Wedding Dress

Imagine a wedding dress that costs a million dollars.
Imagine a wedding dress that allows the wearer to
find her one true love—not always the man she
thinks it is. And then imagine a wedding dress that
brings out all the best attributes in its bride, so that
every man who glimpses her is sure to fall in love.
Karen Toller Whittenburg imagined just such a dress
and allowed it to take on a life of its own in her new
American Romance trilogy, *The Magic Wedding Dress*.
Be sure to catch all three:

March
#621 MILLION-DOLLAR BRIDE

May
#630 THE FIFTY-CENT GROOM

September
#648 TWO-PENNY WEDDING

Look us up on-line at: http://www.romance.net

WDRESS2

HARLEQUIN®

Don't miss these Harlequin favorites by some of our most distinguished authors!
And now, you can receive a discount by ordering two or more titles!

HT #25663	THE LAWMAN by Vicki Lewis Thompson	$3.25 U.S.☐/$3.75 CAN. ☐
HP #11788	THE SISTER SWAP by Susan Napier	$3.25 U.S.☐/$3.75 CAN. ☐
HR #03293	THE MAN WHO CAME FOR CHRISTMAS by Bethany Campbell	$2.99 U.S.☐/$3.50 CAN. ☐
HS #70667	FATHERS & OTHER STRANGERS by Evelyn Crowe	$3.75 U.S.☐/$4.25 CAN. ☐
HI #22198	MURDER BY THE BOOK by Margaret St. George	$2.89 ☐
HAR #16520	THE ADVENTURESS by M.J. Rodgers	$3.50 U.S.☐/$3.99 CAN. ☐
HH #28885	DESERT ROGUE by Erin Yorke	$4.50 U.S.☐/$4.99 CAN. ☐

(limited quantities available on certain titles)

	AMOUNT	$
DEDUCT:	**10% DISCOUNT FOR 2+ BOOKS**	$
ADD:	**POSTAGE & HANDLING**	$
	($1.00 for one book, 50¢ for each additional)	
	APPLICABLE TAXES**	$_____
	TOTAL PAYABLE	$_____
	(check or money order—please do not send cash)	

To order, complete this form and send it, along with a check or money order for the total above, payable to Harlequin Books, to: **In the U.S.:** 3010 Walden Avenue, P.O. Box 9047, Buffalo, NY 14269-9047; **In Canada:** P.O. Box 613, Fort Erie, Ontario, L2A 5X3.

Name:_____

Address: _____ City:_____

State/Prov.:_____ Zip/Postal Code:_____

**New York residents remit applicable sales taxes.
  Canadian residents remit applicable GST and provincial taxes.   HBACK-JS3

Look us up on-line at: http://www.romance.net